AN EERIE CALM...

Jonathan noticed again how quiet it was. No magpies cawed, no leaves rustled overhead. The air was stifling, with no hint of breeze.

Moose barked. Jonathan jumped at the sudden noise. It was Moose's warning bark, the one he used when a stranger knocked on the door. The dog's eyes had a frantic look. He was shaking.

"What's wrong, boy?" Jonathan asked.

Jonathan looked in all directions. He saw nothing unusual. There were still no people and no animals that would startle Moose and set him off. Jonathan listened hard, wondering if Moose had heard something that Jonathan couldn't hear.

Abby stopped walking. "What was that?" she said.

"What was what?"

Jonathan listened. He heard a deep rumbling sound in the distance.

OTHER BOOKS BY PEG KEHRET

Abduction
Cages
Don't Tell Anyone
The Ghost's Grave
I'm Not Who You Think I Am
Nightmare Mountain
Runaway Twin
Searching for Candlestick Park
Stolen Children
Terror at the Zoo

The Pete the Cat Series
Spy Cat
The Stranger Next Door
Trapped

EARTHQUAKE TERROR

PEG KEHRET

PUFFIN BOOKS
An Imprint of Penguin Group (USA) Inc.

PUFFIN BOOKS
Published by the Penguin Group
Penguin Young Readers Group, 345 Hudson Street, New York, New York 10014, U.S.A.
Penguin Group (Canada), 90 Eglinton Avenue East, Suite 700, Toronto, Ontario, Canada M4P 2Y3
(a division of Pearson Penguin Canada Inc.)
Penguin Books Ltd, 80 Strand, London WC2R 0RL, England
Penguin Ireland, 25 St Stephen's Green, Dublin 2, Ireland (a division of Penguin Books Ltd)
Penguin Group (Australia), 250 Camberwell Road, Camberwell, Victoria 3124, Australia
(a division of Pearson Australia Group Pty Ltd)
Penguin Books India Pvt Ltd, 11 Community Centre,
Panchsheel Park, New Delhi - 110 017, India
Penguin Group (NZ), 67 Apollo Drive, Rosedale, North Shore 0632, New Zealand
(a division of Pearson New Zealand Ltd)
Penguin Books (South Africa) (Pty) Ltd, 24 Sturdee Avenue,
Rosebank, Johannesburg 2196, South Africa

Registered Offices: Penguin Books Ltd, 80 Strand, London WC2R 0RL, England

First published in the United States of America by Cobblehill Books, an affiliate of Dutton Children's Books, a division of Penguin Books USA Inc., 1996
Published by Puffin Books, 1998
Reissued by Puffin Books, a division of Penguin Young Readers Group, 2006, 2011

41 43 45 47 48 46 44 42

THE LIBRARY OF CONGRESS HAS CATALOGED THE COBBLEHILL EDITION AS FOLLOWS:
Kehret, Peg.
Earthquake terror / Peg Kehret.
p. cm.
Summary: When an earthquake hits the isolated island in northern California where his family has been camping, twelve-year-old Jonathan Palmer must find a way to keep himself, his partially paralyzed younger sister, and their dog alive until help arrives.
ISBN: 0-525-65226-4 (hc)
[1. Earthquakes—Fiction. 2. Survival—Fiction. 3. Brothers and sisters—Fiction.
4. Physically handicapped—Fiction.]
I. Title
PZ7.K2518Ear 1996
[Fic]—dc20 95-20462 CIP AC

Puffin Books ISBN 978-0-14-038343-0

Printed in the United States of America

For Nancy McGriff, Kathy Schultz, Beth Elshoff,
Desiree Webber, Terri Street, Chapple Langemack,
Ruth Shafer, James Fox, Linda Hoke, Linda Mapes,
and all of the others who give time and talent
to produce awards for children's books.

EARTHQUAKE TERROR

CHAPTER ONE

The deserted campground seemed eerie, like a ghost town. It's too quiet, Jonathan thought. Where is everyone?

Even though the purpose of a camping trip was to get away from the city, it seemed unnatural to hear no boat motors, no radios, and no human voices except for his family.

On previous camping trips there had always been a few other people around, even late in the year like this. Today the only sounds were the cawing of an occasional magpie and the dry leaves crackling underfoot as Jonathan and his golden retriever, Moose, walked along the trail.

Apparently the Palmers were the only family in Northern California who chose to visit Magpie Campground that day. Of course it was a Tuesday, which made a difference. Campgrounds were always busier on weekends. Still, Jonathan thought, it was weird, and he walked faster despite the heat.

The weather seemed more like July than October. Maybe everyone else chose to stay in their air-conditioned homes and watch the World Series game on television. Jonathan would have preferred that, too, but his parents had insisted he come along on the overnight outing. Today and tomorrow were planning days for teachers, so Jonathan did not have school.

"Wait for us, Jonathan."

When he heard his mother's voice, Jonathan stopped. He rubbed the toe of his tennis shoe into the dusty trail, dislodging a stone. *Wait for us, Jonathan. Wait for us, Jonathan.* Jonathan looked back at his parents and sister. Sometimes it seemed he spent his entire life waiting.

Moose tugged impatiently at his leash.

Jonathan picked up the stone and tossed it into the trees. A squirrel chattered its displeasure.

"Sorry," Jonathan said.

Moose sat and scratched his ear with his hind leg. His tags jingled. Jonathan did some leg stretches to keep limber and then glanced down the trail again.

Mr. Palmer had stopped, too, and was looking behind him.

The whole family waits for Abby, Jonathan thought. We have already wasted half the morning, waiting for Abby. He wondered if his parents ever got as frustrated by it as he did. If so, they didn't show it. No matter how long it took Abby to maneuver her walker, they encouraged her to move around by herself, while they waited.

Grandma Whitney said it would be simpler for all of them if Abby used a wheelchair. Abby preferred to crawl. She placed her forearms, from elbow to wrist, on the floor and pulled herself forward, with her legs dragging behind. Because her arms were strong, she crawled quickly and with surprising grace. "Her Marine crawl," Mr. Palmer called it.

Mr. and Mrs. Palmer let Abby crawl only at night, between bathtime and bed, when she was tired and cranky. The rest of the time they insisted on the walker, refusing a wheelchair altogether. They said Abby's leg muscles would grow stronger if she used them and weaker if she didn't.

Jonathan did some knee bends and thought about how vacations used to be. Before Abby's accident, the Palmers climbed mountain trails and slept in sleeping bags under the stars. He remembered two camping trips where he and his parents had hiked for an entire day, with baby Abby in a backpack.

He remembered how good it felt to rest on a rock, high on a hill, and look out over the treetops. He used to push himself to keep up; he sometimes got short of breath.

His sister was born when Jonathan was six, and she had her accident two years later. Now it took more than an hour just to stroll the short, level trail that wound along the riverbank from their campsite to the lake. Now they slept in a small trailer because Abby needed a real bed, with a mattress, not a sleeping bag on the ground.

The Palmers never came to Magpie Campground during the popular summer months anymore, when the lake was a favorite destination for swimmers, and fishermen clogged the riverbanks. It was too difficult for Abby to get around when the trails were crowded; other people were not as patient as her family.

It isn't Abby's fault that her legs are partially paralyzed, Jonathan reminded himself. *She can't help it that she isn't able to walk alone.* He watched as Abby lifted the metal walker and put it down, then leaned on it to balance herself while she stepped forward.

Jonathan's mother walked behind Abby. When Mrs. Palmer saw Jonathan watching, she smiled and waved at him, a signal that he could proceed.

As soon as he reached the lake, Jonathan took the leash off Moose. The big dog immediately splashed into the water, jumping and running along the shore. Jonathan found a piece of driftwood, yelled, "Moose! Fetch!" and threw it into the lake. Moose swam to it, grabbed the driftwood in his mouth, and swam back to shore. He shook the water off his coat, dropped the driftwood at Jonathan's feet, and looked at Jonathan expectantly, as if to say, *Well? Aren't you going to throw it again?*

Jonathan tossed the driftwood again and Moose plunged after it. Jonathan took off his shoes and socks and waded in ankle-deep, curling his toes around the small stones that covered the lake bottom. The cold water felt good on such a warm day, with the sun beating through his T-shirt. Jonathan removed his Giants cap and put it on backward, so the bill would protect the back of his neck while he looked into the water. He was glad his mother had insisted he rub sunscreen on his face and arms before they left the camper.

Behind him, he heard his parents and Abby emerge from the trail.

"Jonathan's in the water," Abby said. "Be careful, Jonathan!" she yelled.

Abby's parents had taken her many times to the public swimming pool near their home, thinking that water exercises would help her leg muscles. Many people can move their arms and legs better in the water, they told her. They can do things in the water that they can't do otherwise.

But Abby had panicked in the pool. No matter how reassuring her parents were, each time she felt the water around her, she grew fearful and refused to let go of the side of the pool. After a few weeks, her parents gave up and quit taking her.

"Come on in, Mom," Jonathan called. "The water feels like a warm bath." It was a long-standing joke between them, dating from a day when three-year-old Jonathan, shivering and blue with cold, had begged to remain in the lake longer, insisting that the water was as warm as his bath.

"Go ahead," Mr. Palmer said to his wife. "I'll help Abby."

Mrs. Palmer sat on a driftwood log, took off her shoes and socks, and rolled up her jeans. While Mr. Palmer helped Abby move her walker along the edge of the water, Mrs. Palmer ran toward Jonathan.

"You lied!" she yelled, as her feet hit the water. "This water is freezing."

"A warm bath," Jonathan replied.

"My feet are turning blue." She pointed to her right. "Look. I see ice cubes floating over there."

Jonathan laughed.

She was only six feet away from him when she went down. Cold water splattered Jonathan and, for a moment, he thought she had done it on purpose—flung herself, clothes and all, into the lake, to swim. He almost belly flopped beside her but the look on her face made him stop short.

"Mom?"

A second ago she joked about ice cubes and now she was sprawled on the lake bottom, with only her head above the water, grimacing in pain.

Jonathan rushed to her side. "Dad!" he yelled.

Mr. Palmer splashed toward them, leaving Abby on the shore.

Mrs. Palmer sat up.

"Are you okay, Mom?" Jonathan asked. He held one hand out to help her up, but she didn't take it.

"My foot just went out from under me," she said.

Mr. Palmer reached them.

"Jack," Mrs. Palmer said softly. "I think I broke my ankle."

Mr. Palmer bent and put his hands under her arms, gently lifting her out of the water until she stood on her left leg, keeping her right knee bent. Carefully, she touched her right toes to the lake bottom. She winced and Jonathan saw that she was biting her lower lip to keep from crying out.

"Don't try to stand on it," Mr. Palmer said. "Jonathan, get on the other side of her."

"What happened?" Abby cried. "What's wrong with Mommy?"

Jonathan quickly moved to his mother's side.

With one hand on Jonathan's shoulder and the other around her husband, Mrs. Palmer managed to hop out of the lake on one foot. Each time she moved, a soft "uuh" escaped from her tightly closed mouth. Slowly they made their way to the driftwood log. Jonathan and Mr. Palmer eased her down until she sat, with her right leg extended in front of her.

The ankle was already swollen.

"We need to get you to a doctor," Mr. Palmer said. "Fast."

"Fast is not a choice," Mrs. Palmer said. "It'll take us an hour to get back to the car and then it's twenty miles to town."

Jonathan saw beads of sweat on her upper lip, and when she wiped them off, her hand shook.

Abby struggled toward them as if she dragged an anchor behind her. Her walker sank an inch into the sandy lakeshore each time she leaned on it and she had to yank upward to lift it enough to move it forward again.

Jonathan watched her approach. Her face was flushed from the heat and the effort. In this emergency, Abby seemed unbearably slow. He turned to his father.

"You could take Mom to town alone," he said. "I'll help Abby on the trail and we'll wait in the camper until you get back."

"We can't leave you out here by yourselves," Mrs. Palmer said. "There isn't even a telephone."

"I take care of Abby at home," Jonathan said, "while you go grocery shopping. This won't be any different. And Moose is with us."

"We would get to the car faster alone," Mr. Palmer said. "Maybe I can carry you."

"Mommy can use my walker," Abby said.

"It isn't high enough for Mommy," Mr. Palmer said. "Thank you, anyway, Abby."

"Go on," Jonathan said. "Abby and I will have lunch and after we eat we'll walk back to camp. By then she'll be ready for a nap."

"Well . . ." Mrs. Palmer said.

"You'll probably be back before she wakes up."

"The sooner we get someone to examine that ankle," Mr. Palmer said, "the better. And Jonathan is perfectly capable of taking care of Abby." He knelt and put his wife's sock and shoe on her left foot. He put the other shoe and sock in his backpack with their lunch, and gave the pack to Jonathan.

"The first aid kit is in the car," Mrs. Palmer said, as she wiped the perspiration off her face. "I believe I'll take some aspirin as soon as we get there."

Jonathan's mother rarely took any kind of medication. He knew her ankle must hurt badly.

"Be careful," Mrs. Palmer said. "When you get back to the camper, wait for us there. Don't go anywhere else."

"We won't," Jonathan said.

"Lock the door after you get there."

"I will," Jonathan said.

"If any other people arrive, wait until we're back to talk to them."

Jonathan nodded.

Mr. Palmer folded his arms across his chest. "Aren't you going to tell them to wash their hands before they eat?" he said.

"I don't like leaving them here alone."

"Neither do I, but it's the best choice. Let's go." He helped his wife up off the log, keeping one arm around her waist while she balanced on her left foot.

Mrs. Palmer put her hand on Abby's cheek. "Abby, you do what Jonathan tells you while we're gone."

"I want to go with you," Abby said. Her lower lip trembled.

"I know you do, sweetie," Mr. Palmer said, "but this time it will be best if you and Jonathan wait for us here. We'll hurry."

"Promise?"

"Cross my heart." Mr. Palmer made an exaggerated *X* across his chest with one hand. Then he picked up his wife and carried her across the sand to where the trail entered the woods.

Just before they started down the trail, Mr. Palmer

stopped and looked back. "It will probably take about three hours," he said. "Even if Mom has to stay at the hospital, I'll easily be back before dinner."

"Don't worry," Jonathan said. "We'll be okay."

Moose loped toward Mr. and Mrs. Palmer.

"Moose!" Jonathan shouted. "Come back."

The dog stopped, looking first at Mr. and Mrs. Palmer and then back at Jonathan and Abby.

"Stay with Jonathan," Mr. Palmer said.

"Here, Moose!" Jonathan called. As the dog ran back to Jonathan, Jonathan yelled, "Good luck, Mom!"

"I want to go with them," Abby said.

"Shh," Jonathan whispered. "We don't want Mom to worry about us. She has enough problems without us along to worry about."

"She'll worry about us if we stay here, too," Abby said.

Jonathan wondered if his dad could carry his mom all the way to the car. How much did she weigh? He thought it was about one hundred and thirty pounds. That was a lot for anyone to carry on a hot day. Probably Dad would have to put her down and have her hop part of the way. It would be slow going, even without Abby.

He watched until his parents disappeared into the trees. If Mom had to break a bone, why couldn't it have happened at home, instead of out on this island, miles from medical help? There was no telephone service here; there wasn't even any electricity.

The camping guidebook referred to Magpie Island as a "primitive facility" which meant the hiking trails and campsites were cleared, but there was no water available and no picnic tables or fireplaces. The rest rooms were only pit toilets.

Primitive is fine, Jonathan thought, as long as there wasn't a problem. He did not want to stay in this isolated place. He did not want to be responsible for Abby.

Beside him, Moose whined. Jonathan put his hand on the dog's head and fought a powerful urge to run after his parents.

CHAPTER TWO

"Is Mommy going to die?" Abby asked.

"No. People don't die from a broken ankle. She might have to wear a cast on her leg for awhile, but she won't die."

"Mommy's NEVER going to die," Abby declared. "Mommy's going to live until she's a million years old."

Jonathan made no comment about that prediction. It seemed safer to change the subject. "Let's play sink-the-ships," he said.

"Okay."

It was a game they had invented last year when they came here at summer's end. Jonathan gathered large brown leaves from the woods. He and Abby stood together at the edge of the water, right where Magpie Creek flowed into the lake, and he handed the leaves to her, one at a time. She dropped them in the lake, where they bobbed and floated like small boats.

When all the leaves were adrift, Jonathan said, "It's time to sink the ships."

He collected a handful of pebbles, gave half to Abby and yelled, "Sink the ships! Sink the ships!" They threw the pebbles at the leaves, trying to make them sink.

Abby clutched her walker with one hand and flung the small stones with all her might. She cheered whenever a leaf went under. Jonathan let her sink most of the leaves, enjoying her excitement.

When the last leaf sank to the bottom of the lake, Abby smiled at Jonathan and said, "I'm hungry."

"Me, too."

He opened the backpack and removed sandwiches, grapes, chocolate chip cookies, and two juice packs.

Moose thumped his tail on the ground when Jonathan also found three dog biscuits.

"I wonder if Mommy and Daddy are in the car yet," Abby said.

"Probably. I'll bet they're driving out of camp right now. Maybe they're already going across the bridge."

In his mind, Jonathan could see his father unhitching the small camping trailer. He pictured the car going along the narrow, winding road that meandered from the campground through the woods. He saw the high bridge that crossed the river, connecting the island campground to the mainland.

He imagined his father driving across the bridge, faster

than usual, with Mom lying down in the back seat. Or maybe she wouldn't lie down. Maybe, even with a broken ankle, she would wear her seat belt. She always did, and she insisted that Jonathan and Abby wear theirs.

Moose cocked his head, as if listening to something. Then he ran toward the trail, sniffing the ground.

"Moose," Jonathan called. "Come back."

Moose paused, looked at Jonathan, and barked.

"Come!"

Moose returned but he continued to smell the ground and pace back and forth.

"Moose wants Mommy," Abby said.

Moose suddenly stood still, his legs stiff and his tail up. He barked again.

"Silly old dog," Abby said.

He knows something is wrong, Jonathan thought. Dogs sense things. He knows I'm worried about Mom. Jonathan patted Moose's head. "It's all right, Moose. Good dog."

Moose barked again.

"I'm hot," Abby said. "It's too hot to eat."

"Let's start back. It'll be cooler in the shade and we can finish our lunch in the camper."

Maybe he could relax in the camper. Here he felt jumpy. He didn't like being totally out of communication with the rest of the world. Whenever he stayed alone at home, or took care of Abby, there was always a telephone at his fingertips or a neighbor just down the street. If he had a problem, he could call his parents or Mrs. Smith next door or even nine-one-one.

Here he was isolated. I wouldn't do well as a forest ranger, Jonathan thought. How do they stand being alone in the woods all the time?

He rewrapped the uneaten food, buckled the backpack over his shoulders, and put the leash on Moose. The goofy way Moose was acting, he might bolt down the trail and not come back.

Jonathan helped Abby stand up and placed her walker in position. Slowly, they began the journey across the sand and into the woods, to follow the trail through the trees.

Jonathan wished he had worn a watch. It seemed as if his parents had been gone long enough to get partway to town, but it was hard to be sure. Time had a way of evaporating instantly when he was engrossed in an interesting project, such as cataloging his baseball cards, or reading a good mystery. But time dragged unbearably when he was in the dentist's office or waiting for a ride. It was hard to estimate how much time had passed since his parents waved good-bye and walked away. Forty minutes? An hour?

Abby walked in front of him. That way he could see her and know if she needed help, and it kept him from going too fast. When he was in the lead, he usually got too far ahead, even when he tried to walk slowly.

While they walked Jonathan planned what he would do when they got back to the camper. As soon as he got Abby settled on her bed, he would turn on the radio and listen to the ball game. That would give him something to think about. The San Francisco Giants were his favorite baseball team and he hoped they would win the World Series.

Jonathan noticed again how quiet it was. No magpies cawed, no leaves rustled overhead. The air was stifling, with no hint of breeze.

Moose barked. Jonathan jumped at the sudden noise. It was Moose's warning bark, the one he used when a stranger knocked on the door. He stood beside Jonathan and barked again. The dog's eyes had a frantic look. He was shaking, the way he always did during a thunderstorm.

"What's wrong, boy?" Jonathan asked. He reached out to pet Moose but the dog tugged toward Abby and barked at her.

"Hush, Moose," Abby said.

Jonathan looked in all directions. He saw nothing unusual. There were still no people and no animals that would startle Moose and set him off. Jonathan listened hard, wondering if Moose had heard something that Jonathan couldn't hear.

Abby stopped walking. "What was that?" she said.

"What was what?"

Jonathan listened. He heard a deep rumbling sound in the distance.

Thunder? He looked up. The sky was bright and cloudless. The noise came closer; it was too sharp to be thunder. It was more like several rifles being fired at the same time.

Hunters! he thought. There are hunters in the woods and they heard us move and they've mistaken us for deer or pheasant. Moose must have seen them or heard them or possibly smelled them.

"Don't shoot!" he cried.

As he yelled, Jonathan felt a jolt. He stumbled forward,

thrusting an arm out to brace himself against a tree. Another loud noise exploded as Jonathan lurched sideways.

He dropped the leash.

Abby screamed.

A bomb? Jonathan thought. Who would bomb a deserted campground?

The noise continued, and the earth moved beneath his feet. As he felt himself lifted, he knew that the sound was not hunters with guns. It was not a bomb, either.

Earthquake! The word flashed across his brain as if he had seen it blazing on a neon sign.

He felt as if he were on a surfboard, catching a giant wave, rising, cresting, and sliding back down again. Except he was standing on dry land.

"Jonathan!" Abby's scream was lost in the thunderous noise. He saw her fall, her walker flying off to one side as she went down. Jonathan lunged forward, arms outstretched, trying to catch Abby before she hit the ground. He couldn't get there fast enough.

The ground dropped away beneath his feet as if a trapdoor had opened. His legs buckled and he sank to his knees. He reached for a tree trunk, to steady himself, but before his hand touched it, the tree moved.

Jonathan's stomach rose into his throat, the way it sometimes did on a fast elevator.

Ever since first grade, when the Palmers moved to California, Jonathan had practiced earthquake drills in school each year. He knew that most earthquakes occur along the shores of the Pacific Ocean. He knew that the San Andreas fault runs north and south for hundreds of miles in California, making that land particularly susceptible to earthquakes. He knew that if an earthquake hit while he was in school, he was supposed to crawl under his desk or under a table because injury was most likely to be caused by the roof caving in on him.

That was school. This was Magpie Island. How should he protect himself in the woods? Where could he hide?

He struggled to his feet again. Ahead of him, Abby lay whimpering on the ground. Moose stood beside her, his head low.

"Put your hands over your head," Jonathan called.

The ground shook again, and Jonathan struggled to remain on his feet.

"I'm coming," he shouted. "Stay where you are. I'm coming!"

But he did not go to her. He couldn't.

He staggered sideways, unable to keep his balance. He felt as if he were riding a roller coaster standing up, except the ground rocked back and forth at the same time that it rolled up and down.

A clump of small birch trees swayed like dancers and then fell.

The rumbling noise continued, surrounding him, coming from every direction at once. It was like standing in the center of a huge orchestra, with kettle drums pounding on all sides.

Abby's screams and Moose's barking blended with the noise.

Although there was no roof to cave in on him, Jonathan put his arms over his head as he fell. The school's earthquake drills had taught him to protect his head and he did it the only way he could.

Earthquake.

He had never felt an earthquake before and he had always wondered how it would feel. He had questioned his teacher, that first year. "How will I know it's an earthquake?" he asked.

"If it's a big one," the teacher said, "you'll know."

His teacher had been right. Jonathan knew. He knew with a certainty that made the hair rise on the back of his neck. He was in the middle of an earthquake now. A big one.

The ground heaved, pitching Jonathan into the air.

CHAPTER THREE

Jonathan hit the ground hard, jarring every bone in his body. Immediately, the earth below him moved, tossing him into the air again.

As he dropped back down, he saw the trunk of a giant redwood tree tremble. The huge tree swayed back and forth for a few moments and then tilted toward Jonathan.

Frantically, he crawled to his left, rushing to get out of the tree's path.

The roots ripped loose slowly, as if not wanting to relinquish their century-long hold on the dirt.

As Jonathan scrambled across the unsteady ground, he clenched his teeth, bracing himself for the impact.

The tree fell. Air whizzed across Jonathan as the tree trunk dropped past, and branches brushed his shoulder, scratching his arms. The redwood crashed beside him, missing him by only a few feet. It thudded down, landing at an angle on another fallen tree. Dirt and dry leaves whooshed into the air, and then settled slowly back down.

The earth shuddered, but Jonathan didn't know if it was from the impact of the tree or another jolt from the earthquake.

With his heart in his throat, Jonathan crept away from the redwood tree, toward Abby. Beneath him, the ground swelled and retreated, like ocean waves. Twice he sprawled facedown in the dirt, unable to keep his balance. The second time, he lay still, with his eyes closed. How much longer would this go on? Maybe he should just lie there and wait until the earthquake was over.

"Mommy!" Abby's shrill cry rose above the thundering noise.

Jonathan struggled toward her again, his heart racing. When he finally reached her, he lay beside her and wrapped his arms around her. She clung to him, sobbing.

"We'll be okay," he said. "It's only an earthquake."

Only an earthquake. He remembered magazine pictures of terrible devastation from earthquakes: homes toppled, highways buckled, cars tossed upside down, and people crushed in debris. Only an earthquake.

"We have to get under shelter," he said. "Try to crawl with me." Keeping one arm around Abby's waist, he got to his hands and knees and began crawling forward on the undulating ground.

"I can't!" Abby cried. "I'm scared. The ground is moving."

Jonathan tightened his grip, dragging her across the ground. A small tree crashed beside them. Dust rose, filling their noses.

"I want Mommy!" Abby shrieked.

He pulled her to the trunk of the huge redwood tree that had uprooted.

"Get under the tree," he said, as he pushed her into the angle of space that was created because the center of the redwood's trunk rested on the other tree.

When Abby was completely under the tree, Jonathan lay on his stomach beside her, with his right arm tucked beneath his stomach and his left arm thrown across Abby. He pulled himself in as close as he could so that both he and Abby were wedged in the space under the big tree.

"What's happening?" Abby sobbed. Her fingernails dug into Jonathan's bare arm.

"It's an earthquake."

"I want to go home." Abby tried to push Jonathan away.

"Lie still," Jonathan said. "The tree will protect us."

The dry forest floor scratched his cheek as he inhaled the pungent scent of dead leaves. He felt dwarfed by the enormous redwood and tried not to imagine what would have happened if it had landed on him.

"Moose!" he called. "Come, Moose."

Beneath him, the ground trembled again. Jonathan tightened his grip on Abby and pushed his face close to hers. A sharp *crack* rang out beside them as another tree hit the ground. Jonathan turned his head enough to peer out; he saw the redwood branches quivering from the impact.

What if the earthquake caused the redwood to move again? What if it slipped off the tree it rested on and crushed them beneath it? Anxiety tied a tight knot in Jonathan's stomach.

The earth shuddered once more. Abby buried her face in Jonathan's shoulder. His shirt grew wet from her tears. The jolt did not seem as severe this time, but Jonathan thought that might be because he was lying down.

Moose, panting with fear, huddled beside Jonathan, pawing at Jonathan's shoulder. Relieved that the dog had not been injured, Jonathan put his right arm around Moose and held him close.

As suddenly as it had begun, the upheaval stopped. Jonathan was unsure how long it had lasted. Five minutes? Ten? While it was happening, time seemed suspended and Jonathan had thought the shaking might go on for days.

The woods were quiet.

He lay motionless, one arm around Abby and the other around Moose, waiting to see if it was really over. The air was completely still. After the roar of the earthquake, the silence seemed both comforting and ominous.

Earlier, even though there were no other people in the area, he'd heard the magpies cawing, and a squirrel had complained when Jonathan tossed a rock.

Now he heard nothing. No birds. No squirrels. Not even wind in the leaves.

He wondered if his parents had felt the quake. Sometimes, he knew, earthquakes were confined to fairly small areas.

Once Grandma Whitney had called them from Iowa. She had seen news reports of a violent California earthquake less than one hundred miles from where the Palmers lived.

"Are you all right?" Grandma cried, when Mrs. Palmer answered the phone. "Was anyone hurt?"

Grandma had been astonished when none of the Palmers knew anything about an earthquake.

After several minutes of quiet, Jonathan eased out from under the tree. He sat up and looked around. Moose, still trembling, licked his hand.

Jonathan put his cheek on the dog's neck and rubbed his ears. He had chosen Moose at the animal shelter, more than six years ago. The Palmers had planned to get a small dog but the moment Jonathan saw the big golden retriever, who was then one year old, he knew which dog he wanted.

Mrs. Palmer had said, "He's too big to be a house dog."

Mr. Palmer said, "I think he's half moose."

Jonathan laughed and said, "That's what I'll name him. Moose."

His parents tried unsuccessfully to interest Jonathan in one of the other, smaller dogs, before they gave in and brought Moose home.

Despite his size, Moose was a house dog from the start, and he slept beside Jonathan's bed every night. They played fetch, and their own version of tag, and Jonathan took Moose for long walks in the county park. In the summer, they swam whenever they had a chance.

When Abby had her accident and Jonathan's parents focused so much of their attention on her, Moose was Jonathan's comfort and companion.

Now, in the devastation of the earthquake, Jonathan again found comfort in the dog's presence. He let go of Moose and looked around. "Wow!" he said, trying to keep his voice steady. "That was some earthquake."

"Is it over?" Abby's voice was thin and high.

"I think so."

He grasped Abby's hand and pulled her out from under the tree. She sat up, apparently uninjured, and began picking leaves out of her hair.

"Are you okay?" he asked.

"My knee is cut." She touched one knee and her voice rose. "It's bleeding," she said, her lip trembling. "You pushed me under the tree too hard."

Jonathan examined her knee. It was a minor cut. He knew that if he made a fuss over it, Abby would cry. He had seen it happen before; if his mother showed concern about a small injury, Abby practically got hysterical, but if Mom acted like it was no big deal, Abby relaxed, too. It was as if she didn't know whether she hurt or not until she saw how her parents reacted.

"It's all right," he said. "If that tiny little scrape is all you got, you are lucky, and so am I. We could have been killed."

"We could?" Abby's eyes grew round.

Quickly Jonathan said, "But we weren't, and the earthquake is over now."

"Where's my walker?" she asked. "What happened to my walker?"

Jonathan stood up. His legs felt wobbly, the way they always did when he got off his skateboard after skating for a long time.

"I'll get it," he said, but when he looked around, he did not see Abby's walker. He didn't even see the trail where she had been standing when the walker was jolted out of her hands. Toppled trees crisscrossed the earth like spilled toothpicks.

Not all of the trees had fallen, but even those that remained standing had lost limbs. The ground was littered with branches of all kinds.

"I want my walker." Abby was near tears again, looking frantically in all directions. "Where is my walker?"

"It's under one of the fallen trees," he said. "I'll find it."

Jonathan began to lift the downed branches, looking under them. In some places, branches were layered three or four deep. Many were too large and heavy to lift; all he could do was dig through the leaves and try to see what was underneath.

"Do you see it?" Abby asked.

"Not yet. But it has to be close by. We were standing right here when the earthquake started."

"No, we weren't. We were over there." Abby pointed about twenty feet from where Jonathan was searching.

He hesitated. She might be right. He couldn't swear which direction they had rolled on the ground, or how far he had crawled, trying to find protection under the fallen tree. And it was impossible to tell where the trail had been. The woods looked the same in every direction: devastated.

He climbed over a pile of branches, making his way toward where Abby pointed. As he continued his search, his mind raced, wondering exactly how much damage the earthquake had done. What about Mom and Dad? Had they made it into town already or were they still in the car when the quake came? What if the road was blocked by downed trees before they got to town? Mom couldn't walk and Dad couldn't carry her through this kind of mess. What would they do?

"Do you see it?" Abby asked.

The earth shuddered again.

"It's come back!" Abby yelled.

Moose barked.

Jonathan crouched, covering his head. It was a single jolt this time, an aftershock. It lasted only five seconds, but that was long enough to send Jonathan's blood racing through his veins. He wondered how many more aftershocks there would be.

When it ended, he waited a few seconds and then, when nothing else happened, he stood and continued his search. He pushed back another pile of branches, bent down, and looked through the tangle of leaves.

"Here it is!" he cried, as he spotted a metal leg sticking out from under a small tree. He lifted the tree and kicked the walker free. It was badly bent, with one leg twisted at a right angle to the others.

When she saw the walker, Abby gasped. "It's broken. I can't use it that way."

"Maybe I can straighten it." Jonathan stood on the bent leg and pulled on the top of the walker with all his might. Instead of straightening, the metal leg snapped off.

Abby looked more frightened now than she had during the earthquake. "What will I do?" she whimpered. "How will I walk?"

Jonathan knew she was dependent on her walker. When she went to sleep at night, it always stood beside the bed, where she could see it as soon as she opened her eyes. When she ate, her walker waited beside the table, where she could reach it.

He felt a rush of empathy, thinking what it would be like to be unable to swing your legs out of bed in the morning and walk unaided to the closet for your clothes. In the same instant, he realized how frustrating it must be to inch slowly along the trail to the lake while your big brother jogs impatiently ahead.

"I want Mommy!" Abby wailed, tears spilling onto her cheeks.

So do I, thought Jonathan.

Another aftershock began, stronger this time. Jonathan felt as if he were standing on a giant accordion whose sides were moving in and out. He dropped to the ground and covered his head until the movement stopped.

CHAPTER FOUR

"I want Mommy!" Abby repeated, louder this time.

Jonathan could tell she was on the verge of losing all control. He said, "Mom and Dad will come back as soon as they can."

But when will that be? he wondered. What condition is the road in, between the bridge and Beaverville? Even if the earthquake had been confined to Magpie Island, it meant that Dad could not drive back to the campground. He would have to leave the car and hike from the bridge to the camper.

Mom, of course, was not likely to return at all. She would either be in the hospital or at home, a fact which Jonathan decided not to share with his sister.

There was no way to know how much of the road was

blocked by fallen trees. It might be hours before his father returned. Or it might be days.

Jonathan had never felt so alone. He wished he had not offered to stay behind. He didn't want to be in charge of Abby, not in an earthquake.

Abby wailed louder.

"It won't do any good to cry," Jonathan said. "You'll just give yourself a headache."

He knew he sounded cross but he needed to think, and Abby's yowling did not help.

Her wails subsided, becoming long, jerky open-mouthed breaths. She lifted the hem of her T-shirt and blew her nose on it.

If I were alone, Jonathan thought, I would hike the road to the bridge and make sure Mom and Dad made it off the island.

But he was not alone.

Dad had said, "Jonathan is perfectly capable."

Jonathan took a deep breath, consciously trying to calm himself. Mom and Dad were counting on him; they believed he could take care of his sister. He wondered what they would do in this situation.

I need to do two things, he decided. First, keep us safe. Second, don't let Abby panic.

He had already kept them safe once, by lying under the fallen tree while other trees crashed down around them. He might even have saved their lives. He had thought fast in an emergency, and had done the smart thing. Compared to that, it should be a breeze to keep a six-year-old from crying.

"When we get to the camper," Jonathan said, "I'll play *Go, Fish* with you."

Abby closed her mouth, blinking at him through her tears.

"Four games of *Go, Fish*," Jonathan said.

"I can't go back to the camper without my walker." She wiped her tears on the back of her hand.

"I'll help you walk. You can hold onto my arm and we'll go slowly."

Abby thought a moment. "Ten games of *Go, Fish*," she said.

"Six."

"Okay. Six."

He took both her hands and pulled her to her feet.

"The trail is gone," Abby said. "Which way are we supposed to go?"

Jonathan looked around. She was right. He wasn't sure where the trail used to be. It would be difficult enough to get Abby back to the camper without her walker; it would be disastrous to go in the wrong direction.

Sweat trickled down the back of his neck.

The sun. That's how he could tell. The sun was on his back earlier when he ran ahead of Abby and his parents, on his way to the lake. The sun was directly overhead while they played sink-the-ships. By now, it would have moved farther west so it would be on his back again, as he returned to the camper.

He glanced down at Abby's frightened face.

"I know which way to go," he said calmly. "East. Away from the sun." He offered Abby his arm and she clung to it.

He stepped forward, with the sun filtering through the trees on his back. Abby stepped with him, her eyes sweeping the trees ahead.

They had gone only a few yards when a huge fallen tree blocked their way. The side of the trunk was up to Abby's waist.

"We'll have to climb over it," Jonathan said. "It will take too long to go around." Seeing the look of disbelief on Abby's face, he added, "I'll help you. Put your back next to the tree. Rest your legs against it."

Abby did. Jonathan quickly climbed over the tree, turned and leaned across it. Putting his arms under Abby's arms, he clasped his hands across Abby's chest.

"The Great Abby Elevator will now pull you up and over," he said. "Just go limp, like your Raggedy Ann doll."

He felt her tense muscles relax. He pulled up and back, until she was sitting on top of the fallen tree. She turned sideways and Jonathan lifted her legs, one at a time, so that they lay on top of the trunk.

Abby turned some more and slid on her bottom across the tree trunk until her legs dangled down the other side. It was easy, then, for Jonathan to steady her while she slid down again.

When she was safely on the ground, Jonathan guided Abby to a standing tree.

"Lean against the tree," he said, "while I clear a path for us."

Abby put her stomach against the tree and leaned forward.

"Hi, tree," she said, wrapping her arms around it. "Would you like a hug?"

While Abby talked to the tree, Jonathan cleared six feet of path. Then he helped Abby walk forward to another tree. Again, Abby leaned against the tree while Jonathan pulled fallen branches off the trail, making a path wide enough for them to walk side by side.

Slowly, they made their way through the woods. Since Jonathan had to clear most of the trail of fallen branches, they stopped frequently. Clear another six feet; help Abby walk. Clear and help Abby; clear and help Abby.

Moose jumped easily over most of the fallen trees, and went around the others.

"When we get to the camper," Jonathan said, "we'll stay there. There's plenty of food and water. Even if it takes Mom and Dad awhile to get back, we'll be okay. We can listen to the radio while we play *Go, Fish*."

He could stand to play six games of *Go, Fish* if he listened to the ball game at the same time. He wondered if the Giants and *A*'s had felt the earthquake at Candlestick Park. Probably not. San Francisco was almost one hundred miles away and he didn't think earthquakes covered that much territory.

He would get Abby safely into the camper and then he could listen to Game One of the World Series while she took a nap. There might even be a newsbreak, telling about the earthquake. He would learn how strong it was and whether it did any damage beyond Magpie Island.

"I'm tired," Abby said. "My legs hurt."

"We can't stop now. We have to get back to the camper."

The earth shuddered again. Another aftershock. Moose whimpered. Abby and Jonathan clutched each other and waited for it to pass.

He wondered how long they had been walking. It seemed hours. Abby was slow when she had her walker; it was far worse now. They climbed over several more fallen trees. Each time, it was harder for Jonathan to hoist Abby up and over. Each time, his muscles strained and he grunted from the effort.

His right knee was swollen and discolored where he had landed on it after being tossed in the air. I need an ice pack, he thought. I need to put my foot up and stay off that leg.

Jonathan wondered again what the road into camp was like. Probably crews with chain saws would have to come and cut through fallen logs before Dad could drive the car back into camp. How long would that take? At least the bridge to the mainland, arching high above the Tuscan River, would be clear of trees.

Abby stopped. "I can't go any more."

"I think we're almost there. See that big oak tree up ahead? We passed that when we first started down the trail this morning. I remember because it reminded me of the oaks in Grandma's yard."

Was it only this morning? It seemed days ago that they had started out, the five of them, for an ordinary picnic lunch at the lake.

"I can't walk. My legs hurt."

"Then I'll carry you. Piggyback." Jonathan bent over. "Put your arms around my neck," he instructed. Abby did.

Jonathan tried to straighten up but he couldn't lift her off the ground. His back ached as he strained to raise his shoulders. Sweat trickled from the back of his neck into the corners of his mouth.

He tried three more times, but she was too heavy, and he was too weary.

CHAPTER FIVE

Another aftershock rumbled beneath them. It was a small shake, not even enough to make Jonathan lose his balance.

"Make it stop!" Abby cried.

Even small shakes, Jonathan thought, create fear, because we don't know until it's done that it *is* small. Every tiny tremor might be the start of another big one.

"Let's eat the rest of our lunch," Jonathan suggested. Maybe food and a short rest would give both of them new energy.

At least he didn't have to worry about saving any food for later; there was plenty to eat in the camper. Dad always said Mom packed enough to feed an army.

They sat on a log and Jonathan opened the backpack. He handed Abby a sandwich bag.

"It's all smashed," Abby said. She held the flattened sandwich bag by two fingers, as if it were something rotten. The sandwich looked as if someone had used a rolling pin on it. Tuna salad oozed out from between the slices of bread and clung to the plastic bag.

"I must have squashed the backpack, when we were under the tree," Jonathan said. "Sorry."

The grapes were a mush of stems and juice.

Abby wrinkled her nose. "Yuk," she said.

"I'm going to eat my sandwich anyway," Jonathan said.

When Abby hesitated, he added, "You can lick the tuna off the sandwich bag."

Abby brightened. Her favorite treat was a chocolate cupcake but whenever she started licking the frosting or crumbs off the wrapper, Mrs. Palmer said it wasn't polite to lick the wrapper, and made her stop.

Abby opened her sandwich bag, turned the bag inside out, and enthusiastically licked all the tuna salad off.

Jonathan broke his sandwich in two and gave one half to Moose.

"I'm sure that's the only big oak tree we passed," Jonathan said. "Our camper will be just beyond that. Once we get there, you don't have to walk any more. And when Mom and Dad come, they'll take us home and they'll get you a brand new walker, even better than your other one."

Abby opened her bag of broken cookies and started licking the crumbs. "When we get to the camper, I'm going to take a little nap," she said.

It was the first time he had ever heard his sister voluntarily suggest that she go to sleep. Usually, she insisted she wasn't tired, even while she rubbed at her half-closed eyes.

"I'll rest, too," he said, "and listen to the ball game." Maybe cheering for the Giants would keep his mind off the fact that he and Abby were alone in an isolated campground, and he had no clue how soon his parents would arrive to take them home.

When they finished eating, Jonathan said, "Let's go, Abby."

"No. I'm tired. I want to stay here."

"After we get to the camper, you can rest as long as you want. You'll be more comfortable on your bed than you are here, and you'll have Raggedy to sleep with."

When they got back to the camper, he would feel safe again. He would get out the first aid kit and put some disinfectant on Abby's scrapes, and on his own scratched arms and legs. He could get Abby settled in her bed, lock the door, ice his knee, and wait for Dad to come for them.

"I'm thirsty," Abby said.

"You can have a drink of water as soon as we reach the camper."

"I don't want water."

"Milk, then."

"I don't want milk, either."

"Okay. You can have whatever you want." Jonathan was determined not to argue.

"What if I want coffee?" Abby said and then giggled. "What if I want a pineapple milk shake?"

"There's no ice cream in the camper. I'll make some lemonade."

"You said I can have anything I want and I want a pineapple milk shake."

He knew she was just being ornery. She loved lemonade. "You can have a pineapple milk shake when we get home. You can have three pineapple milk shakes, all in one day."

"Okay. I'll have lemonade now."

Jonathan cleared more branches from what used to be the trail and hoisted Abby over yet another fallen tree. Moose clambered over, too.

"We're almost there," Jonathan said. "When we get to the oak tree, we curve to the right and our camper will be there waiting for us."

"When we get there, can I have a chocolate cupcake?"

"Yes. And you can lick the wrapper all you want."

Lemonade and chocolate cupcakes. Jonathan could imagine what his mother would think of such a snack. She always urged them to eat apples or bananas if they were hungry, and when they were thirsty, she suggested water or orange juice.

Well, this was an emergency and if sweet food would keep Abby happy until their parents returned, that's what he would give her. He might have a chocolate cupcake himself. He might even lick the wrapper.

Near the oak tree, there were fewer branches down. The original trail was almost clear and Jonathan's spirits rose. He had *thought* they were going the right direction but now he was sure of it.

Anticipating the end of their struggle, he walked faster.

Moose ran forward until the leash was taut and then doubled back, as if urging them to hurry. Abby clutched Jonathan's arm and managed to keep up with him. They followed the trail as it curved to the right. Around the bend, they stopped.

The trail was completely blocked by roots. An enormous redwood tree had been torn from the ground. Clumps of dirt clung to its roots, which stretched twenty feet across and twenty feet high. There was no way they could climb over this; they would have to go around it.

"Wait here," Jonathan said. "I'll find the best way for us to get around this tree." He helped Abby sit on the ground and then, climbing through underbrush and fallen branches, he made his way around the huge root system. He wondered how many years the redwood had stood in this spot. He marveled that any force, even an earthquake, had been strong enough to uproot it.

He shoved through some huckleberry bushes, wishing that he had worn jeans instead of shorts, and long sleeves rather than a T-shirt.

Moose hung back, watching him.

"Stay," Jonathan said. He let go of the leash, needing both hands free to push his way through the brush.

"Hurry!" Abby's small voice sounded scared. He knew she didn't like to be left alone.

"I am. I'm almost there."

He reached the far side of the roots and looked ahead to see how far they were from the camper. A prickle of horror ran down the back of his neck and into his arms and legs.

The redwood tree had landed on their camper.

Bile rose in Jonathan's throat. He swallowed fast, trying not to throw up. He stepped closer, staring at the wreckage.

The edge of one black tire stuck out from under the tree. The rest of the camper was flattened like an aluminum can in the recycling bin. Even with the camper underneath it, the tree was only a few inches off the ground.

Their supplies and equipment were smashed inside the camper. All the things he had counted on to help them while they waited to be rescued were gone. He and Abby had no food and no water. They had no beds, no extra clothing, no first aid kit.

Nothing.

Mentally, Jonathan walked through the camper, remembering the contents. Sleeping bags and pillows, my Yahtze game, long forks for roasting marshmallows, folding chairs to use around the campfire, Mom's books, Dad's wood carving tools, Abby's doll, my radio, Moose's basket.

My homework! Jonathan smiled. It would be the most unusual excuse ever for not turning in an assignment: "A huge redwood tree fell on top of my homework."

How can I make jokes, Jonathan wondered, when I've just lost everything I need to survive this disaster? But he knew that if he didn't joke about his homework, he would be hysterical with worry.

Moose plunged through the huckleberries and ran to the

camper. With his nose to the ground, he sniffed all the way along the side of the tree. Whining, he turned and sniffed all the way back again, the leash dragging behind him.

"It's gone, Moose," Jonathan said. "Everything's gone, even your dog food."

Jonathan picked up the leash. He patted Moose's head. What am I going to do now? he wondered.

Jonathan wanted to run. He wanted to vault over the fallen trees and run like the wind and leave this shuddering, destructive, unpredictable piece of Earth far behind him.

Just me and Moose, Jonathan thought, closing his eyes. We could run across the bridge, run off the island, run to safety. We'll run to town, find Mom and Dad, and never again think about a camper smashed in an earthquake.

"Jonathan?" Abby's shout drifted over the redwood's roots.

Jonathan opened his eyes, knowing he could not run.

"I'm coming," he yelled.

"Did you find the camper?"

"Yes!"

He stared at a small strip of yellow awning that was visible along the trunk of the tree. Mom always said the awnings made the camper look cheerful, "like a clump of buttercups, blooming outside our windows."

Yes, he thought. Yes, I found the camper. But it isn't going to do us any good.

CHAPTER SIX

Moose whined again.

Jonathan leaned against the tree trunk, wondering what to do. His head pounded, the scratches on his arms and legs stung, and every muscle in his body ached from the strain of lifting Abby over the fallen trees. He tried to figure out some kind of plan.

He knew he had to have a specific course of action in mind before he told Abby about the camper. Otherwise, she was sure to come unglued and, as tired as she was, she'd probably never stop crying. He felt like crying himself.

The thick redwood bark was cool against his back. He closed his eyes, pretending his parents were there to tell him what to do.

First things first, Dad always said. Decide what's most important and then do that before you do anything else. Most important, Jonathan thought, was to get rescued but he didn't know what he could do about that.

First things first. Food. Water. Shelter. Food wasn't crucial yet, since they had just eaten and he still had the two smashed sandwiches that were meant to be his parents' lunch.

Water *was* important. Abby was already asking for something to drink and his own mouth felt dry as dust. He thought of the gallon jugs of bottled water his dad had carefully packed in the camper.

"Probably more than we'll need," Dad had said, "but the worst thing that could happen would be to run out of water."

Not the worst thing, Dad, Jonathan thought. The worst thing is to have an earthquake that smashes the entire camper, water jugs included. Jonathan licked his lips, tasting the salt of his perspiration.

He still had two juice packs, intended for his parents. I'll save them as long as I can, he decided, in case we don't get rescued right away.

There was plenty of water in the river but, even though it ran swiftly, it was probably too polluted to drink.

He wished he knew whether Mom and Dad had made it to town before the earthquake hit. If they did, Jonathan should wait by the camper, and help would get there soon, or at least as soon as possible.

But what if they didn't make it? What if the road was blocked by fallen trees and Mom was still sitting in the car while Dad walked to town? Even worse, what if one of the trees had landed on the car? Jonathan shuddered. Maybe Mom and Dad needed help just as much as Jonathan and Abby did.

The longer he waited, the more thirsty and tired he and Abby would be. Before too long, they would be hungry, as well. He did not want to stay here and wait for help that might never come.

I need to follow the road, Jonathan decided. I'll hike the route that Mom and Dad would have driven. If they made it off the island, I won't find anything, and I can turn back when I reach the bridge, and wait with Abby for help to arrive.

If I *do* find them—well, if that happened, he would decide what to do then. He could always hike off the island by himself, if he had to. He could cross the bridge and walk to Beaverville, the closest town.

Either way, Abby would have to wait where she was. He could go ten times faster alone than he could go with Abby.

She won't want to wait, Jonathan knew. She'll cry herself into a snit if I leave her alone for long. He would have to leave Moose with her and hope that Moose would not take off after a squirrel or a chipmunk.

Maybe he could rig up some kind of shelter, so that Abby would have a special place to wait while he was gone. If he made a game of it, like playing house in the woods, she could lie down in the shelter and sleep while he walked to the bridge and back. He knew she was tired. She might sleep the whole time he was gone. With luck, Moose would stay with her and sleep, too.

His plan decided, Jonathan started back around the roots.

"We can't use the camper," he told Abby, trying to sound matter-of-fact. "This big tree smashed it."

Abby's bottom lip quivered but before she could cry, Jonathan hurried on. "Aren't we lucky that we weren't in it, when the earthquake came? And we're lucky now, too, because you don't have to walk any farther. We're going to make a little house right here in the woods." He glanced quickly around, and then pointed at the last tree they'd climbed over, a large maple. "That tree trunk is going to be one wall of our house."

"The camper's smashed?" Abby said.

Jonathan nodded.

"What about my Raggedy?"

She had left her favorite doll, the one she slept with every night, in the camper. "Raggedy is still in the camper," he said, "but I can't get her out because the tree is too heavy."

"I want Raggedy!"

"My radio was in the camper, too. I can't get my radio out, either."

Abby nodded and was quiet, as if she didn't mind losing her doll as long as Jonathan also lost something important.

"It's going to be fun to build a little house in the woods," Jonathan said, forcing himself to sound cheerful.

"How are we going to make a house? We don't have a hammer."

"We don't need a hammer. We'll use small trees that fell during the earthquake. And we'll make beds out of pine branches."

Abby looked doubtful. "What about my chocolate cupcake?" she said. "You promised I could have a chocolate cupcake."

"You can have it later." Much later, Jonathan thought.

"I'll have it for dinner," Abby said.

Dinner, Jonathan knew, would be another squashed sandwich and a bag of cookie crumbs, but he didn't say that.

"I'll have chocolate cupcakes for breakfast tomorrow, too," Abby declared.

Jonathan nodded. By then—oh, surely by then—his father or a rescue crew would come for them. "I'd better get started on our house," he said.

"I want to help. I want to build the house, too."

"You can be the boss. You sit right there and I'll ask you questions."

Jonathan looked around for trees that were big enough to use and small enough that he would be able to move them. He found three small alders and dragged them, one at a time, to where Abby sat.

"Which one shall we do first?" he asked, and Abby pointed.

After stripping off as many of the lower branches as he could, he laid the root end of the alder on top of the downed maple's trunk. He did the same thing with the other two alders.

Next he gathered pine and cedar boughs. Some of these he put on the ground, as a bed for Abby and Moose. The rest he laid on top of the alders, forming a crude roof. He placed the alder branches that he had removed across the far end of the shelter, propping them up to form a back wall.

The shelter was shaped like half a tent, with an opening at one end.

"There," he said, stepping back to admire his work. "It's a fine looking house, if I do say so myself."

"It isn't very big," Abby said. "We won't be able to stand up in it."

"We don't sleep standing up," Jonathan said. "Crawl in and try it."

Abby crawled under the roof and lay face down on the pine boughs. "It's too prickly. The branches scratch my cheek."

"Lie on your back. Smell the cedar?"

Moose sniffed the branches around Abby's toes.

"It smells like Mommy's blanket chest," Abby said as she rolled on to her back.

Jonathan patted the branches beside Abby. "Here, Moose," he said. "Lie down."

Moose walked in a circle beside Abby and then flopped beside her. She put an arm on his side and Moose thumped his tail.

"Stay," Jonathan said.

Abby sat up. "I'm thirsty," she said. "I want a drink of water before I go to sleep."

Jonathan hesitated. Maybe if she thought he was going after water, she would wait without so much fuss.

"All right," he said. "I'll go look for some water."

Abby patted the dog. "You can use the red bucket, to carry the water in."

Her words made him realize that she still did not comprehend that they had lost all of their equipment. "The bucket was in the camper," he said. "I can't get it."

"I want to go along and look for water, too."

"You can't. It would take too long." He saw her lip start to quiver again.

"It's not fair," she said.

"You're right. It isn't." Jonathan squatted beside the shelter and looked at his sister. "I'm sorry, Abby," he said, and he truly meant the words. "You'll have to wait here for me. Moose will stay with you. You can be in charge of Moose."

"I'm Moose's boss?"

"That's right." He leaned in the opening of the shelter and put Moose's leash, which had been dangling on the ground, in Abby's hand. "Hold on tight," he said, "and talk to Moose so he won't be scared."

"But *I'm* scared."

"Pretend you aren't. Pretend you're brave and that will help Moose."

"I'll take care of you, Moose," Abby said, "until Mommy and Daddy come back."

"I'm going now," Jonathan said. "Lie down and close your eyes. Smell the pine smell and think about what Santa might bring you this year."

"Hurry?"

"As fast as I can." Which won't be very fast, Jonathan thought, given the condition of the trail. As he turned to go, Abby started to cry.

"I don't want to stay alone. What if the earthquake comes back?"

The same thought had occurred to Jonathan. He knew more aftershocks were likely. Smaller earthquakes often followed a large one. Sometimes they weren't so small. Another huge jolt could come any minute. But he couldn't sit around doing nothing, waiting for disaster to strike.

"I wish I had Raggedy," Abby said.

"I wish you did, too." She looked so young, lying there. She was so helpless, without her walker. What if there was another earthquake before he returned? What would she do?

His worst fear kept popping into his mind. *What if Mom and Dad didn't make it off the island?* Any hope of a rescue depended on his parents being where they could send help. But what if they hadn't made it that far before the earthquake hit? What if they were also trapped on the island?

With a broken ankle, Mom wouldn't be able to climb over fallen trees. She couldn't hike across the bridge.

Stop it, he told himself. Quit being a pessimist. Maybe they *did* make it off the island in time. Maybe they've already alerted the police or the road department or whomever would need to authorize a crew to get us out of here. Maybe help was already on the way.

Maybe. Everything was *maybe*. He needed to know, and the only way to find out was to walk along the road from camp to the bridge and find out if his parents were trapped there or not.

"I'm going now," he said, and left quickly, before Abby could protest again.

Jonathan went around the redwood, passed the crushed camper, and headed toward the bridge. The dirt road was visible in places but he had to climb over downed trees and push through tangles of fallen branches in order to follow it.

He tried to hurry but, even without Abby, his progress was slow. He wished he and Abby had walkie-talkies or some other way to communicate.

Periodically, he snapped a twig into a *V* shape and laid it down, pointing behind him. It would be easy to get lost, now that most of the road was covered. He had to make sure he could find Abby again.

An uneasy stillness hung over the island and the air seemed heavy and thick. Perspiration soaked Jonathan's T-shirt and trickled down his forehead.

He wasn't certain how far it was to the bridge. A mile, perhaps. Maybe a little more than that. A mile's hike was nothing, under ordinary circumstances. But this road, in its present state, was far from ordinary.

The earth shuddered again, a small jolt this time, but enough to put Jonathan's nerves on edge. He hoped Abby was asleep. She might not feel it, if she was asleep.

He pushed on, jogging whenever there was a clear space, which wasn't often. His eyes searched the woods ahead, dreading what he might see. The farther he got without finding a smashed car, the more hopeful he was.

As he neared the approach to the bridge, the trees gave way to low shrubs. He could hear the river now and with fewer fallen branches, the road was visible again. Encouraged, Jonathan hurried on. Mom and Dad must have made it off the island.

He ran the last fifty yards, up the embankment to the start

of the bridge. He had not found the car, so he knew Mom and Dad had made it off the island before the earthquake. Maybe Dad was already on his way back to Magpie Island.

When he reached the edge of the bridge itself, he stopped running and gasped.

The bridge went only partway across the river. The steel structure stretched across half the water and then ended abruptly. The other half of the bridge looked like a giant water slide. It lay at a steep angle from the opposite shore straight down into the water of the Tuscan.

The bridge had been snapped in two by the earthquake.

CHAPTER SEVEN

Dad won't be back.

The knowledge filled Jonathan with alarm. He stood at the edge of the embankment, looking at the broken bridge, and knew there was no way Dad's car or any other vehicle would come to the island now. Not today. Not tomorrow. Not for many weeks, or maybe even months.

There was no way for Jonathan and Abby to walk off the island, either. They would have to wait for someone in a boat or a helicopter to rescue them.

Jonathan's knees felt weak and he plopped onto the ground, as all hope for a fast rescue vanished.

Jonathan looked into the rushing water. Had Mom and Dad made it safely across the bridge before the earthquake tore it in two? If a car had been on the bridge when it broke, the car would have plunged into the river, would have sunk quickly to the bottom.

A person with a broken ankle would have a hard time climbing out of a car that was underwater. A person with a broken ankle would probably not be able to swim to shore. A person . . .

Stop it! Jonathan told himself.

He turned and started back to Abby. Fear formed a hollow place in his chest.

Until now, Jonathan had thought if no one came to rescue them, he would walk across the bridge and hike to Beaverville and bring help back for Abby. He would have been a hero. "Courageous boy walks twenty miles to save sister. Details at six."

Well, forget the hero bit. That plan was no longer an option.

Jonathan felt far more helpless, knowing he had to wait for help to come to him, than he had felt when there was some action he could take.

Weighed down by this new disaster, Jonathan walked more slowly on the return trip. Twice, the V-shaped twigs served to direct him. Each time he came to one, he snapped it into several pieces. He had to be sure he didn't start going in circles, following the same twig more than once.

Moose heard Jonathan coming and came to greet him. Jonathan knelt and hugged the dog, burying his face in the soft fur, inhaling the familiar doggie scent.

"Some boss," he whispered. "She didn't even hold on to your leash."

Moose licked Jonathan's arm.

Abby was asleep. Wearily, Jonathan crawled into the shelter and lay beside her.

The sun was low in the sky. Where were Mom and Dad? They made it off the island but that didn't necessarily mean they had made it to the hospital. It was twenty miles from the bridge to Beaverville and that road could be as impassable as the road between the bridge and the campground.

He had not found a smashed car on the island, but maybe the car was smashed somewhere else. Or maybe it was at the bottom of the Tuscan River.

If his parents could send help, they would. Jonathan knew that. He also knew they might not be able to send help, and if that were so, Jonathan must somehow help himself.

I need to make a signal that can be seen from the air, Jonathan decided, some sign that we're here. That way, even if Mom and Dad haven't made it to town yet, someone in a plane might spot the signal and realize we need help.

A fire, perhaps? Smoke would be seen a long way off, and a fire would be noticed even after dark. He had learned in Cub Scouts how to create sparks by rubbing stones together. He could gather twigs and start a fire.

He crept out of the shelter without waking Abby, and quickly gathered a pile of dry leaves. It was easy to find twigs for kindling and he soon had a tepee of twigs built over his leaf pile. But as Jonathan bent to pick up a larger branch, he realized how dry the forest floor was. There had been no rain for months.

He couldn't build a fire, not with the forest so dry. One wayward spark and the whole island would go up in flames. Jonathan kicked his pile of twigs and leaves, scattering them in a circle.

He needed a clearing. He needed a big open space where he could take large sticks and spell out H-E-L-P.

The lakeshore! There was a wide stretch of beach between the end of the trail and the edge of the lake. It would be perfect. He could make the sign and start a fire, too, to draw attention to the sign. He would build the fire close to the lake, and put wet sand all around it to keep it from spreading.

Jonathan scooped up some of the dry leaves and twigs and stuffed them into his backpack. He gathered an armload of inch-thick sticks, for firewood.

He hurried through the woods toward the lake, following the path he had cleared earlier when he and Abby returned to camp. Alone, he covered the distance quickly.

He saw the big redwood tree that he and Abby hid under during the earthquake. Just beyond it, he saw water.

Jonathan stopped and stared. The earthquake hadn't hit until he and Abby were far down the trail, well away from the lake. He shouldn't be able to see water already. Yet there it was.

Jonathan dropped his sticks and plunged through the brush until he reached the big redwood. He scrambled up on the trunk and stood, looking across what had been the trail.

The lake was different than before. Closer. Water now covered the forest floor where he and Abby had first struggled to walk. Broken branches bobbed on the surface.

Jonathan slid down the far side of the redwood. Splash! His feet landed in an inch of boggy water. He slogged forward, curious to see where the water came from. Had the earthquake rearranged the lake?

He continued walking until the water was ankle deep. Then he climbed partway up a maple tree and looked west. With so many trees down, the forest was not so dense and he could see clearly. What he saw sent chills down the back of his neck.

The sandy beach was underwater. The junction of stream and lake, where he and Abby played sink-the-ships, was underwater. And a large portion of Magpie Island was underwater.

The lake was much bigger than it had been before. It was far larger even than it got in winter when the Tuscan River was at its deepest.

In his mind, Jonathan saw the layout of Magpie Island as it looked on the map. It sat in the middle of the wide Tuscan River. One small stream, Magpie Creek, flowed across the island into Magpie Lake, and then flowed out the other side where it rejoined the Tuscan.

If Magpie Lake was suddenly expanding, the river must have changed. What had happened? Had harmless Magpie Creek suddenly overflowed its banks?

Jonathan watched the water inch closer. What if the earthquake had created a natural dam of fallen trees? What if the Tuscan was flowing into Magpie Creek and from there into Magpie Lake, as it always had, but no water was flowing out on the other side? There would be no place else for that water to go except to overflow on the island.

Jonathan took a step backward. How big would the lake get? How long would a dam hold?

How close to the campground would the water come?

Magpie Island was only a few miles wide and the only bridge connecting the island to land was broken.

The Tuscan River was a huge river—big enough for houseboat rental companies to flourish. If it was now flowing into Magpie Lake, the lake might get big enough, deep enough, that the whole island would eventually be underwater. Magpie Island would disappear, possibly forever.

Water lapped at the tree trunk below him. Jonathan stared down at it. The lake was definitely moving toward him.

Jonathan climbed down the tree and sloshed through the woods toward his sister. He could not spell out H-E-L-P, when there was no longer any land between the lakeshore and the woods.

He needed someone to talk to, someone who could give him some advice. He needed to tell someone that Magpie Lake had overflowed its banks, and he and Abby were trapped in its path and he wasn't sure what to do next.

The thought of tidal waves jumped into his mind. He remembered pictures on the classroom bulletin board of a tidal wave following an earthquake. In Jamaica, he thought.

His teacher had talked about an earthquake in Alaska, too, where parts of the ocean floor rose fifty feet.

But Magpie Island was sixty miles from the ocean. Surely a tidal wave wouldn't surge that far upriver, causing a flood, and wiping out everything in its path.

Would it?

Jonathan wished he had been more interested last year when his teacher had talked about earthquakes. Mrs. Higgins had even offered a chance to earn extra credit by doing a report on earthquakes, but it had been in the spring, at the start of baseball season, when Jonathan didn't have a lot of extra time.

He took deep breaths, trying to stay calm. Surely help would arrive soon. Even with the bridge out, Mom and Dad would make sure that he and Abby were rescued. By now, rescuers were probably on the way.

Maybe we'll have to be airlifted in a helicopter, Jonathan thought. *That would be exciting.*

He didn't care how they got out. He just hoped it would happen soon. If it didn't, and the water kept coming . . .

Jonathan ran faster. He couldn't just wait for rescuers to come. What if the water got there first?

Abby was awake when he returned to the shelter.

"Where's my drink?" she asked.

Jonathan opened the backpack, threw out the dry leaves he had gathered, and gave Abby one of the two remaining juice packs.

He had planned to save his parents' juice until he was

desperate, but Abby was thirsty and she would be certain to have a tantrum if she didn't get something to drink.

I'm desperate now, Jonathan thought. The river is flooding and half the island is underwater.

And Abby can't swim.

He opened the last juice pack and carefully poured some into his cupped hand for Moose, who lapped it eagerly.

Jonathan drank the rest himself as the thought repeated itself in his brain. Abby can't swim.

CHAPTER EIGHT

Trees float.

He had seen whole logs riding on top of the water in Lake Washington when he visited his cousins in Seattle last year.

We need a raft, Jonathan decided. He would lash some saplings together and make a raft.

Jonathan found four young trees of approximately the same length. One at a time, he dragged them to the clearing near Abby. After breaking off as many limbs as he could, he lined the trees up, side by side. If he could hold them together, they were wide enough for Abby to lie on. He'd give anything for the coil of clothesline that he knew was just inside the door of the camper. He needed to tie the trees together. But how?

He picked up one of the thin branches he had snapped off and stripped all the leaves from it. Then he tried to wind the branch around two of the trees, but the branch kept breaking. It wasn't going to work.

What he needed was rope or wire or even some long strips of a sturdy material.

He remembered the awning. Quickly, he returned to the flattened camper and tugged on the yellow canvas that stuck out from under the tree. He braced his feet and pulled as hard as he could but the awning did not tear.

Jonathan wiped the sweat from his forehead on the bottom of his T-shirt. He fingered the T-shirt fabric. He could tear it into strips but he knew it was not heavy enough to hold the trees together, once they were afloat.

Forget the raft idea.

"I want to play school," Abby said. "I want to be the teacher."

"Okay."

"Get out your songbook," Abby said. "We're going to have music class."

Jonathan sat on the ground and pretended to look at a songbook. He would keep Abby happy while he tried to think what to do next.

Abby began. "Itsy-bitsy spider went up the waterspout."

Jonathan joined in. He felt as if he were having a dream. He and Abby weren't really sitting alone in the wreckage of

Magpie Campground, next to what used to be their camper. There wasn't really river water creeping like a cat across the forest floor toward them, getting deeper by the minute. The whole situation was unreal.

"Down came the rain," Abby sang, "and washed the spider out."

Jonathan wished she had chosen a different song. He wasn't too eager to think about anything, even a spider, getting washed away.

Abby rocked from side to side as she sang her favorite song. Her shadow rocked with her across the ground.

The sun was low in the sky now. Dad had said he would be back by dinnertime. But Dad didn't know there was going to be an earthquake.

"Up came the sun . . ."

Thud.

Jonathan stopped singing. "What was that?"

"And dried up all the rain," Abby trilled.

"Shh! Be quiet a minute."

"*I'm* the teacher," Abby scolded. "You can't quit singing in the middle of the song. You have to mind me and we haven't finished our music lesson."

Thud.

There it was again. It came from behind them, from the west.

This time, Abby heard it, too. Her bossy expression vanished. Fear made her voice soft. "Is it the earthquake again?" she said.

"I don't think so." Jonathan stood up. He walked a few yards, and then scrambled up on a large fallen tree. He looked around, trying to figure out what the noise was.

Thud.

That time, he saw where the noise came from. To his left, one of the toppled trees shifted, bumping hard against another tree. Beside the two trees, brown leaves from the forest floor floated slowly toward him.

Water trickled around the tree's roots and inched closer. How could the water be so near already? It was less than half an hour since he'd seen the water's edge, several blocks down the trail. If it had moved this far so quickly, across the whole width of the island and with all the fallen trees and debris in its path, it wouldn't be long before it swept across the campground, covering the entire island.

Jonathan slid off the tree and hurried back to Abby. "We're going to sit on top of the redwood tree," he said.

"I want to finish my song."

"We will. But we have to get as high as we can. The lake's flooding. I'm going to push some smaller trees over next to this big one, to make steps. Then we can climb up them, and sit on top of the tree."

The trees he had tried to use for a raft were too small. He grabbed one of the alders he had used for their shelter and pulled it past the redwood roots.

"You're wrecking our house!" Abby cried.

"I have to. It's faster than finding new trees for the steps."

Something in his voice quieted her protests. She sat silently and watched.

The redwood had no branches for about twenty feet above the roots, so he was able to pull the alder parallel to the trunk. When it was as close as he could get it, he dragged the other two alders over. He positioned one of them next to the first, and piled the other on top, creating a step. It was hard work and when they were in place, the step they provided was less than two feet high. He needed a lot more than that if he expected to get Abby on top of the redwood.

There wasn't time to construct adequate steps. "Abby," he said, "we are going to climb up those roots."

Abby gave him an astonished look. "How?" she demanded.

"We'll use the roots like rungs on a ladder. You go first. Hang on tight to a root and I'll help you get your feet up."

"We can't do that. It's too high."

"I know it's high. That's why we have to get up there."

"I'll fall."

"No, you won't. I'll stay right beneath you, to be sure."

"I don't want to climb up there."

"Neither do I but the river has flooded and the water's coming this way and we need to get as high as we can."

"How could the river flood? It hasn't rained all summer."

"Maybe the earthquake shifted the water's path. Or maybe trees fell and created a dam and so the water flowing into the lake has no way to get out. I'm not sure what is causing it, but I do know the water is coming this way and we can't just sit here and wait."

As if to prove him right, a tongue of water licked out

from under the tree. Abby stared as the dry ground grew damp.

"I don't like the water," Abby said. "Make it go away."

"Let's start climbing," Jonathan said.

He guided Abby to the base of the roots. "Put your hands up as high as you can reach and find a place to hold on," he said.

Abby put her hands up and felt for something to grasp. Her fingers closed around a piece of root.

"Hold tight and I'll lift your feet up," Jonathan said.

He put his hands on Abby's left ankle and directed her shoe to a large root that was thigh high. He put her second foot beside the first one and pushed on her bottom while she straightened her legs.

Abby clung to the root. "Good," Jonathan said. "That's really good. Now put your hands up higher again."

Abby let go with one hand, keeping her face pressed close to the roots. Her fingers slowly explored the bottom of the tree.

"Go left," Jonathan said. "There's a big one above you to the left."

"Which way is left?"

He tapped her left ankle. "That way."

Her hand moved left until her groping fingers closed around the big root. Her right hand followed. Jonathan again found a higher place for her feet and helped her straighten her legs.

This put Abby high enough that now he needed to start his own climb. It was going to be tricky to hang on himself and still help her move upward but he didn't see any other choice.

Abby stretched her arm up, feeling for another handhold. Her fingers knocked small clumps of dirt loose and they tumbled down, hitting both children on the heads.

"I'm getting dirt in my hair," Abby complained.

"So am I. It doesn't matter. Keep climbing."

"My arms are tired."

"Mom and Dad will be really proud of you for doing this."

Abby's hand found another root. "I'm ready to move my feet," she said.

Jonathan leaned into the root system, hoping his feet would not slip, and let go with his hands. Once again, he was able to lift Abby's feet, one at a time, and position them on a higher root.

"We're almost halfway there," he said. "We're going to make it."

"Halfway!" Abby wailed. "Is that all? I can't do this; it's too hard."

"Would you rather drown?" His own fear and fatigue cut his patience short.

"No."

"All right, then. Keep climbing. Pretend you're the itsy-bitsy spider and you're climbing up the waterspout."

Root by root, they inched straight up the bottom of the tree. Balls of dirt continually rolled down on top of them. One caught Jonathan in the eye just as he looked up to see where Abby's hands were. He blinked furiously, trying to wash the dirt away but his eye felt scratchy and irritated. He kept it closed, hoping the moisture would build up enough to cleanse his eye.

"I'm ready for you to move my feet," Abby said.

"Just a second. I have dirt in my eye." He wished he had some water to splash on his face and rinse out his eye. What a joke, Jonathan thought. Here I am frantically trying to escape the water and at the same time wishing I had some.

After a minute or so, the eye felt better. Squinting to protect his eyes from more dirt, he found a higher spot for Abby's feet and then hoisted himself up another notch.

He was about six feet off the ground now and Abby was another four or five feet above him. He leaned his head back, trying to see what Abby was doing with her hands. If they could just make it to the top of this tree, they would be safe from the rising water for a long time.

"Keep going," he called. "You're doing great!"

Below them, Moose whined. I'm sorry, Jonathan thought. I don't want to leave you behind.

Maybe, after he and Abby got on top of the tree, Moose would be able to climb the roots, too. If I call him and encourage him, he might make it.

With her next step up, Abby was high enough to see over the redwood's roots. When she saw the squashed camper, she gasped. Clearly, she had not understood until then the magnitude of their loss.

"Raggedy's killed," she cried and burst into tears.

"Hang on," Jonathan said. "I'm going to move your feet again."

Abby continued to weep for her lost doll. Jonathan let her cry. He didn't have time or energy or patience to try to calm his sister. He was too busy trying to save her life. He positioned her feet a notch higher.

"Pull yourself up," he shouted. "We're almost to the top."

Before she could respond, the tree roots shifted.

"Jonathan!" Abby screamed, as her feet slipped off the roots. Her legs dangled helplessly.

The huge root mass tipped sideways, and then rolled back.

Below them, Moose barked his warning bark, deep and loud.

"Hang on," Jonathan yelled but the aftershock was too strong. The fallen tree lurched upward and sank back down again so swiftly that both Abby and Jonathan lost their grips and tumbled to the ground.

Jonathan hit first. Abby landed beside him. Clods of dirt from the roots rained down around them.

Jonathan lay still, waiting to see if the aftershocks would continue. When they did not, he said, "Are you all right?"

Her answer was a whimper. Tears rolled down her face.

Beside them, Moose shook the dirt out of his coat.

"I don't think I broke anything," Jonathan said, as he slowly flexed his arms and legs. "What about you?"

"I'm getting wet," she whispered.

Only then did Jonathan realize that he was lying in an inch of water.

She'll drown, Jonathan thought. I have to get her out of here or she will drown.

CHAPTER NINE

Jonathan pulled the alder trees away from the side of the redwood. First they were a house, then they were steps, and now they were going to be boats.

"It's my turn to be teacher," Jonathan said as he selected the two biggest alders. "Today you're going to have a riding lesson, only instead of a pony, you'll learn to ride a tree."

It might work, Jonathan thought. If she lies on her stomach and puts both arms around the tree trunk, she should be able to hang on and keep her head above water.

Abby scowled and stuck out her bottom lip. "It's still my turn to be teacher," she said. "We didn't finish the song."

"You can have a turn next. You can have two turns, but this is important, so listen carefully. We have to hold on to something that won't sink. Like these tree trunks." Jonathan pointed to the alders whose branches he had removed. "We each get to choose one of these trees for our own. Which one do you want?"

Abby looked at the trees. "I don't want one."

"Listen, Abby. The whole island is flooding and you need a tree to ride on in the water."

"Why is there a flood?" she said. "It didn't rain."

"The earthquake caused the flood."

"I don't want to be in a flood. I want my cupcake. You promised me that if I kept walking, I could have lemonade and a cupcake."

"I didn't know the camper was going to be wrecked. Now, which tree do you want? If you don't choose, I'll choose for you."

Abby pointed to the tree closest to her. "That one."

"Good choice. This is now your very own personal tree." He dragged the tree over to where Abby sat. She patted it.

Jonathan thought it was large enough to support Abby but he would need a bigger tree, something that would keep both him and Moose afloat.

He spotted one about twenty feet away.

"I pick that one," he said. He tried to pull the tree closer to Abby but it was too heavy. Instead, he dragged her tree next to the one he had chosen and then helped Abby walk to it. His tennis shoes squished as he sloshed through the water.

"Watch me. This is what you need to do."

Jonathan lay on his stomach on top of his tree, with his

armpits on the tree trunk. "Keep your arms around the tree, like this," he said. "No matter what happens, don't let go. The tree is your friend and will help you stay above the water."

Abby said nothing.

"Do you understand?"

"My shoes are getting wet."

"We're going to ride the trees now," Jonathan said. "We're each going to lie on our own tree. You lie down on yours and I'll lie on mine and we'll hold tight. The trees will be our boats, if the water gets too high."

"What's my tree's name?"

"You get to name it. It can be anything you want. You can name my tree, too."

"My tree is Charlotte and yours is Wilbur."

"All right," Jonathan said. She could name it Dracula, for all he cared. "Lie down on top of Charlotte," he said.

"I can't. My tree is too low."

Jonathan put his hands under Abby's armpits and eased her down into a sitting position. Then he helped her lie flat along the length of the tree, with her cheek resting on the bark. As he did, he was acutely aware that she would not be able to get up off the tree by herself. He would need to stay with her.

"Put your hands on Charlotte's trunk and hold on."

Abby did.

"No matter what happens," Jonathan said, "don't let go of your tree. It isn't just a tree any more. It's your boat."

The water covered his shoes now.

"I want Mommy and Daddy to come back."

"They're trying to come, but it's going to take awhile. The road is blocked and the bridge is out."

"Out where?"

"It broke. The bridge fell down."

Abby raised her head and smiled. "That's what happened in London," she said, and she began to sing. "London bridge is falling down, falling down, falling down."

She's so little, Jonathan thought. She's so little and helpless and she has no idea how much trouble we're in.

"London bridge is falling down, my fair lady."

The water was ankle deep and Jonathan feared it might be a long time before they were rescued. The road toward the bridge on the other side of the island was probably blocked by fallen trees. It could be hours before anyone knows the bridge is gone.

If he and Abby floated away from Magpie Island, even a helicopter might have trouble spotting them. And if it did spot them, how would it land in a river?

Maybe he should put Abby on his tree and try to stay together. But he needed to keep Moose with him and he was afraid their combined weight would be too much to allow the small tree to float. No, he decided. Best to each take a tree.

Abby's tree moved.

"You're floating already," Jonathan said.

Abby quit singing. "This is fun," she said.

Some fun, Jonathan thought grimly, but he'd rather have Abby think it was a game than to have her screaming in terror.

"My boat is moving," Abby said. "Charlotte is swimming in the water."

"Hang on," Jonathan said. "Wrap your arms around Charlotte and hang on." Fear rose in his throat. The water was moving too quickly; it was getting deep too fast. At this rate, the entire island would be underwater long before anyone had a chance to rescue them.

Would Abby hang on? Would she be able to, even if she tried? He needed a way to tie Abby to the tree, so she couldn't fall off.

Jonathan looked at Moose's leash. If he unleashed the dog, he could use the leash to strap Abby to the tree. But what about Moose? If they were about to float down the river on these trees, as Jonathan expected, he needed a way to pull Moose back to the tree, if Moose fell off. And if they somehow made it to shore, he would need the leash there—to keep Moose from running after a wild animal or bolting in fear if there were more aftershocks.

Jonathan's head pounded. He was tired of making decisions. It was too hard to know which action to take when the choices might mean life or death.

If he strapped Abby to the tree, she would not be able to get off, even if she needed to. What if she floated close to shore and had a chance to grab a tree branch and pull herself to safety? Abby's arms were strong; it was only her legs that didn't work right.

If she were strapped to the tree, she might not be able to save herself, if she had the chance.

He left the leash on Moose.

He lay stomach-down on his tree and put one hand on the ground, ready to wrap it around the tree as soon as the water was deep enough. He put his other hand on Abby's tree, just above her head, and gripped the bark with his fingers. If he could keep the two trees together, he would be able to keep Abby from panicking.

"Charlotte is going to float down the river," Abby said.

"So is Wilbur. We're both going for a boat ride." Jonathan tried to sound excited and happy but his voice came out strained. His tree moved beneath him; he, too, was now afloat.

Abby started to sing. "Row, row, row your boat, gently down the stream."

Jonathan closed his eyes. *Please, God,* he prayed. *Please let someone find us soon.*

"Sing with me," Abby said. "Do a round, like Mommy does." She began the song again.

Jonathan rested his cheek against the bark on the tree and, at the appropriate time, joined his sister's song.

"Merrily, merrily, merrily, merrily, life is but a dream."

Some dream, he thought, as the trees bobbed in the rising water. This was worse than any nightmare he'd ever had.

Moose stood beside Jonathan's tree. The water was up to the dog's belly.

"Come on, Moose," Jonathan said. "You'll have to share my tree."

He sat up, straddling the tree trunk, and, using both hands, hauled Moose on to the tree. Moose's paws slipped off and Moose splashed back on to the ground.

Jonathan tried again. This time, he kept his arms wrapped around Moose's middle. "Sit," he commanded. "Sit on the tree."

Instead of sitting, Moose lay down with his nose toward the top end of the tree and his tail toward Jonathan. Quickly, Jonathan moved forward and lay with his chest on Moose's back. He could hold Moose and hang on to the tree at the same time.

Once it reached them, the water rose fast. One minute their trees rested on the ground and then, only a short time later, they were floating in water so deep that when Jonathan put his right hand down, he could no longer feel the forest floor.

His left arm curved around the bottom side of his tree with Moose's leash around his wrist.

With his right hand, Jonathan clutched Abby's tree, trying to keep it from floating away from him.

"Hang on tight," he reminded Abby. "We might not be able to stay together, so no matter where your Charlotte boat goes, hang on to it."

Abby's head jerked up and she looked at him. "I want to stay with you," she said, clearly close to tears again.

"I'll stay as close as I can."

"I want Moose on my boat."

"No," Jonathan said. "Moose has to stay with me." Abby

would never be able to manage the dog on her own. Moose weighed more than she did.

The sun painted the sky gold and then pink and, finally, a deep orange as it dropped below the horizon.

Their trees bumped the redwood's roots, bounced backward, bumped again. Each time, they hit higher. Eventually, they floated around the roots, and over the trunk. The camper was no longer visible. Even the bright yellow awning had disappeared beneath the water.

"I'm scared." Abby's voice was a tiny whisper.

She's too little to do this, Jonathan thought, and too weak.

The song leaped into his mind: Itsy-bitsy Abby, climbed up the waterspout. Down came the rain and washed poor Abby out.

No! She won't get washed away, Jonathan thought. I can't let her be washed away.

But no matter how fierce his determination, Jonathan knew, deep down, that what happened now was beyond his control.

"I want to go home," Abby said.

CHAPTER TEN

The water rose swiftly.

All around them, small trees and branches bobbed like plastic toys in a giant bathtub. At first the trees seemed to float in a random pattern but as the water deepened, they moved in a single direction.

Jonathan realized the trees and branches and other debris were floating toward the setting sun.

Once again, Jonathan pictured Magpie Island on a map but this time he saw it in context with its surroundings. He saw the Tuscan River, not only as it flowed around the island, but as it continued its course due west to the Pacific Ocean.

If he had guessed correctly that the earthquake had created a natural dam which caused the stream across the island to overflow, it meant that he and Abby were not in the small section of river that flowed into the lake where they had played sink-the-ships. They were in the Tuscan itself, the wide, deep river that flowed past Beaverville and Kendra, the two small towns that stood between the island and the coast.

Maybe this is good, Jonathan thought. If we can stay on our trees while we float past the towns, surely someone will spot us from shore.

"I have to go potty," Abby said.

"Go in your pants."

"What?" Astonishment made her voice shrill.

"You heard me," Jonathan said. "We can't leave our boats. And even if we could, there isn't any bathroom. If you need to go, you'll have to go where you are."

"You want me to wet my pants?"

"They're wet anyway, from the river."

Abby was quiet.

In spite of his growing fear, Jonathan smiled. No one had ever suggested such outrageous behavior before and he knew Abby was considering whether or not to take his advice.

Dusk was brief; darkness settled quickly over the island. Their predicament seemed worse, somehow, in the dark. More dangerous. They couldn't be easily seen now, either from shore or from the air.

"I did it." Abby's voice was low. "Don't tell Mommy."

"Mommy won't care," Jonathan said.

"It feels warm."

Moose shifted, his feet slipping on the wet tree.

"Easy, boy," Jonathan said. "Lie still."

"I want to go home," Abby said. "I don't like my boat."

"I want to go home, too, but there isn't any way to do that until Mom and Dad send someone to get us."

"I don't like all this water." She sounded scared. "It's worse than the pool."

Jonathan wondered if she had just realized what was happening. "I don't like it, either," he said, "but our boats will keep us safe."

Abby began to cry.

I have to keep her calm, Jonathan thought. If she panics, she'll forget to hold on.

Jonathan started to sing again. "Itsy-bitsy spider climbed up the waterspout."

Abby listened for a moment and then joined in.

If we get out of this alive, Jonathan thought, I will never again sing about itsy-bitsy spider.

His hand ached from trying to hold on to Abby's tree. In the dark, he couldn't tell how deep the water was but they were moving steadily now. Faster than before. There was more space between their trees and the other trees that were floating, as if the river had widened, making room for its passengers.

The songs were the only way to keep Abby from crying so, while his own fear rose as fast as the water, Jonathan continued to sing.

"Out came the sun and dried up all the rain . . ."

A larger tree slammed into the root end of Jonathan's tree, jolting him sideways. Moose splashed into the river.

Jonathan let go of Abby's tree and grabbed his own to keep from falling off. Moose swam beside the tree. He put one paw up, trying to climb back on, but with no ground under his hind legs to push against, he couldn't make it.

Jonathan leaned into the water, put his arm under Moose's chest and lifted. Moose scrambled back on to the tree.

The tree bobbed and jerked. Jonathan clung to it until it stabilized.

When he reached for Abby's tree, he couldn't find it.

"Hold out your hand," he cried. "This way." He groped toward her in the dark, splashing the surface of the water. He could make out her shape; she was drifting away from him. He leaned toward her until he nearly rolled into the water. He could not reach her.

He unsnapped Moose's leash and, holding the handle in his right hand, flung the clasp toward Abby, as if he were fly-fishing.

"Grab the leash," he called. "It's in the water. Find it and hold on."

"I can't find it!"

The clasp sank. Jonathan pulled it back and tried again, flinging the clasp toward Abby's tree. That time, she grabbed it.

"Hang on to the leash," Jonathan said. "It will keep us together."

"I'll try."

It was easier to hold the leash than it had been to try to

hold on to her tree. Maybe, he thought, this will work better. He tugged on the leash, trying to move the trees closer together.

"You're pulling me off," Abby said.

Jonathan quit tugging.

"I can't see you very well," Abby said. "It's too dark."

"The moon will be out soon."

"I want my night-light. I want my pink blanket. I want Raggedy."

"I'm going to teach you a new song." Jonathan tried to think what songs he knew that Abby didn't. The only one he could come up with was the one his baseball team sang on the bus en route to games: "Ninety-nine bottles of beer on the shelf."

He knew his parents would not appreciate it if he taught his six-year-old sister a song about beer. On the other hand, that song would last a long time and keep Abby calm.

He changed the lyrics and began. "Ninety-nine Raggedy Anns on the shelf; ninety-nine Raggedy Anns. If one of the dolls should happen to fall, ninety-eight Raggedy Anns on the shelf."

By the time he got to ninety-five, Abby had caught on and was singing with him. She didn't know how to count backward so she waited for him to sing the correct number each time and then she joined in. They sang all the way down to one Raggedy Ann on the shelf, and then back up to ninety-nine again.

His tree was bobbing about less, floating more smoothly.

The moon rose, spreading a dim light. Raising his head from the tree, Jonathan looked around. There was water everywhere except far to his right, beyond Abby. In that direction, he saw several bright spots. The brightness was orange and yellow, lighting the sky.

Fire.

Jonathan counted five separate bright areas. Five fires. The dark outlines of buildings were silhouetted against the fire closest to him.

Beaverville is burning, Jonathan realized.

There were no other lights, which meant the electricity must be gone. But there would still be people. People would be there, fighting the fires. They might even be on the banks of the river, dipping buckets of water to use on the fires.

"We're going to call for help," Jonathan said. "Maybe someone on shore will hear us. I'll count to three, and we'll yell together. One. Two. Three. HELP!"

Abby's voice joined his and they screamed together, over and over. "Help! Help!" Then they listened, to see if there was any response. They heard no answering shouts.

Jonathan tried to gauge how far they were from shore. He guessed it was twice the distance from home plate to the center field wall. He was a strong swimmer. He could probably make it, despite the swift current. Moose would make it, for sure. Maybe he and Moose should swim to shore and then someone in a boat could go after Abby and bring her back.

Even as he made the plan, he knew he wouldn't carry it

out. He couldn't leave Abby floating down the river alone. She would be terrified. And without Jonathan to distract her with singing, she would probably get hysterical.

What if she slipped off her tree or was knocked off? At least if they were together, Jonathan might be able to save her if she fell in. By herself, Abby would have no chance.

"One, two, three," Jonathan counted. "Help!" they yelled together. "Help! Help!"

Their shouts faded into the darkness. Could anyone on shore hear them? Was there anyone on shore? Maybe Beaverville had been evacuated. If so, where were Mom and Dad? They had been headed for the emergency room at Beaverville Hospital but maybe the hospital wasn't functioning. Maybe the hospital was burning. For all he knew, most of Beaverville was a pile of rubble.

The shoreline changed. The glow of the fires faded away like the taillights of a passing car.

Beaverville was behind them. Blackness took its place.

"Mommy didn't hear us," Abby said.

"We'll try again at the next town."

"I'm cold. I want my Barney sweatshirt."

For an instant, Jonathan was annoyed. What did she expect him to do, swim back to Magpie Campground, dive under the river, lift the giant redwood with one hand, grab her sweatshirt off the hook, and swim back? "I'm not Superman," Jonathan muttered.

"When we get home," Abby said, "let's make popcorn."

Jonathan's annoyance vanished. She's only six, he reminded himself. She doesn't really understand what is happening to us.

"Popcorn sounds great," he said.

Jonathan knew there was another town, Kendra, still ahead on the bank of the Tuscan. Maybe they would float closer to shore by then. Maybe someone in Kendra would hear their cries.

And maybe not.

CHAPTER ELEVEN

Mrs. Palmer screamed.

Mr. Palmer clutched the steering wheel and slammed his foot on the brake. Trees crashed around them as the car bucked like an untrained horse.

They had just crossed the bridge from Magpie Island to the mainland when the earthquake hit. Without warning, the entire car rose six inches off the road and bounced back down again.

Mr. Palmer turned off the engine but the car kept moving, swaying from side to side and rocking from back to front at the same time. The Palmers leaned forward in their seats, with their hands on their heads, while the earth pitched and rumbled and shook. The quake went on and on.

"We have to go back," Mrs. Palmer said, when it was finally over. "We must get the children."

Mr. Palmer got out of the car and looked around. The road was buckled in several places; trees were down everywhere. He walked behind the car to the bend in the road and looked back toward the island. His heart drummed loudly as he returned to the car.

"We can't go back," he said. "The bridge collapsed."

Mrs. Palmer looked through the windshield at the trees blocking the road. "We can't drive to town, either," she said. "You'll have to walk to Beaverville for help. I'll wait here."

Her ankle throbbed. The movement of the earthquake had made her legs bounce, and several times the broken ankle had slammed into the car door. She hoped she would not pass out from the pain.

"I don't like to leave you," Mr. Palmer said.

"There's no choice."

He nodded. He looked at his wife and saw his own fear reflected in her eyes. Were Jonathan and Abby hurt? How long would it take for help to get to them?

"Get help for Jonathan and Abby first," Mrs. Palmer said. "I can wait. They may not be able to."

He nodded. "I'll hurry," he said.

It was not so easy to hurry. He couldn't just run along the road to town; he had to climb over downed trees and step around fallen branches.

Half a mile from the car, power lines hung across the road. The wooden power pole tilted at a forty-five-degree angle while the lines drooped downward. The wires hissed and sparks flew out. Mr. Palmer walked half a city block out of his way to get past the wires without touching them.

He hoped they didn't start a forest fire. This area was heavily wooded and there had been no rain all summer. He added the power lines to his mental list of emergencies to deal with as soon as he got to town.

Or did this mean there would be no telephone service in Beaverville? Maybe all the power and telephone lines were out of service. It might not be so easy to arrange a rescue for Abby and Jonathan and another for his wife.

He wiped the sweat from his forehead and plunged on toward Beaverville. Fear surrounded him like a winter fog. His body stayed warm from the physical exertion but inside, his heart felt chilled.

Three hours later, he saw a house, set back from the road. He pounded on the door. A fat, balding man opened the door.

"I need help," Mr. Palmer said.

"Don't we all?"

"My kids are alone on Magpie Island and my wife's in the car back by the bridge with a broken ankle. I need to use your telephone."

"Won't do you any good," the man said. "Phone's out. Power's out. Water mains are broken." He opened the door wider. "You're welcome to come in and wait with me and my wife. We can offer you a peanut butter sandwich but that's all."

"Thanks, anyway," Mr. Palmer said. "I'll go on into

town. There must be some sort of emergency headquarters. The Red Cross or the National Guard or someone must be coordinating rescue efforts."

"Good luck," the man said.

"Thanks. I'm going to need it."

As Mr. Palmer continued on the road toward Beaverville, it grew dark. Blisters bubbled on both of his heels. He hoped Jonathan had sense enough to wait in the camper. Abby would fall asleep in a place she was accustomed to.

He smelled the town before he saw it. Smoke hung in the air, making it difficult to breathe. He coughed and held his arm up to his face, trying not to inhale the smoke.

As he climbed a small hill, he saw an orange glow ahead.

At the crest of the hill, Mr. Palmer stopped. Fire!

Flames licked skyward as he gazed down at the town. He saw five separate fires in different parts of Beaverville.

The road down the hill into town was free of debris. Mr. Palmer ran toward the fires. At the bottom of the hill, a group of people milled in the street, watching one of the fires. Mr. Palmer couldn't believe that they were just standing around watching, instead of trying to put the fire out.

"Get water!" he yelled, as he ran toward them. "Get the fire department!"

The group turned to him.

"There isn't any water," a woman said. "All the main water lines broke. We hauled river water in buckets for awhile but we weren't nearly fast enough and we gave up. It was like trying to put it out by spitting."

A man in a baseball cap added, "The fire department is just as helpless as we are. The gas line broke, too, and the gas is feeding the flames."

"Half the buildings in town are on fire," the woman said, "and the other half are knocked off their foundations."

"Are there any emergency services?" Mr. Palmer asked.

"At the high school," someone replied. "People whose homes were destroyed are staying there."

"What about medical help?"

"That's at the school, too. The hospital was evacuated."

Mr. Palmer asked for and received directions to the high school. As he started off, a young man touched his shoulder.

"Anything I can do to help you?" the young man asked.

"My wife's in our car, back near the bridge to Magpie Island. I think she has a broken ankle."

"My name's Kenny," the young man said. "I've got a chain saw and a four-wheel-drive vehicle. Be glad to try to get through to her, if you want to go with me and help clear the road."

"Yes," Mr. Palmer said. "I'd be grateful for that. But first I need to alert the authorities that my children are alone on Magpie Island."

"Are you sure?"

"We left them in our camper while I drove my wife to the hospital. After the earthquake hit and knocked the bridge out, we couldn't go back after them. It will take a boat or a helicopter to get them off the island."

"I heard on the radio a few minutes ago," Kenny said, "that Magpie Island is gone."

"Gone! How could it be gone?"

"The earthquake shifted the flow of the river and the island flooded over and disappeared."

"No," Mr. Palmer said. "No! Not Jonathan and Abby. Oh, please, no!"

"I'm sorry, Sir." Kenny put his arm around Mr. Palmer's shoulder. "We can go to the school and you can hear it for yourself, if you like."

"I believe you."

"Shall we go find your wife?"

Mr. Palmer started to follow Kenny, then stopped. "No. Not yet," he said. "I have to let someone know that Jonathan and Abby are missing. There must be search planes or helicopters. How else would they know the island disappeared?"

"Not much chance of two kids surviving if the whole island's gone," Kenny said softly.

"Maybe they got off the island," Mr. Palmer said. "Maybe they found a boat or something else that floats. Jonathan's a strong swimmer and our dog was with him; maybe he and Moose got Abby to shore."

As he spoke, he knew he was babbling. He saw the pity in Kenny's eyes and knew the young man thought grief was making him grasp at impossibilities.

Maybe I am, he thought. Maybe there's no hope that Jonathan and Abby survived. But I can't give up without trying to find them.

Wearily, he walked toward the high school.

CHAPTER TWELVE

Abby never made it to Kendra.

As they began "Twenty-three Raggedy Anns on the shelf" for the second time, Abby's tree collided with the remains of an old fishing pier. The wooden pier, unused for a dozen years, jutted several hundred feet out from shore. Buoys warned boats to stay away.

The earthquake caused the pier to shift and sink so that it lay just below the surface of the river.

Abby's tree floated between two buoys and hit the top of the last post on the pier.

The collision jarred Abby and sent her tree spinning sideways away from Jonathan's. She dropped the leash and clutched her tree. "My boat hit something!" she cried.

"Hang on!" Jonathan yelled. "Put both arms around Charlotte and hang on."

Jonathan put his right hand in the water and paddled hard, trying to turn his tree toward Abby. The current was too strong. Even though the tree turned slightly, it continued to float rapidly forward. Abby seemed to have stopped moving.

"Stay with me," Abby called. "Hold my hand!"

"I can't. But you can still hear me. We'll be able to sing even better if we each hold tight to our own tree." To prove it, Jonathan started singing again. "Twenty-three Raggedy Anns on the shelf; twenty-three Raggedy Anns."

Although Abby kept singing, the sound of her voice grew faint. Jonathan realized that her tree was not floating as fast as his was. She had somehow been knocked out of the main current and was either drifting aimlessly or was floating toward shore.

He raised his head and looked back.

"Abby?" he called. "Where are you?"

"I'm here. Back here!"

Her voice seemed far behind him. Her tree must not be moving. Something had stopped her. When he looked toward the sound of her voice, he saw so much floating debris in that part of the river that it was difficult in the dim moonlight to pick out which dark shape in the water was Abby. Whatever had caused Abby's tree to stop moving forward, had caused other flotsam to stop there, too.

Jonathan debated. Should he abandon his own tree and try to swim back to Abby? But the town of Kendra was still ahead and with it the chance that someone would hear or see him.

There were no towns along this part of the river. Even if he and Abby got out of the current and made it to shore here, there would be no one to help them. And there was no way for Abby to walk miles to town.

It's better, he decided, to try to get help as fast as possible, rather than to stay behind with Abby.

"Stay with Charlotte," Jonathan shouted. "No matter what happens, stay on your tree."

"Come back!" Abby cried, an edge of hysteria in her voice. "Stay with me."

"I can't. But I'll be back to get you."

"Where are you going?" she called.

I wish I knew, Jonathan thought. He yelled, "I'm going for help. I'll be back for you as soon as I can. Keep singing! Sing to Charlotte."

"Jonathan! Come back!"

"Sing, Abby. Sing the Raggedy song."

"Don't leave me. Come back! Please, Jonathan! I'm scared!"

You aren't the only one, Jonathan thought, I'm more scared than I've ever been in my life.

She quit calling and began to sob. Her voice grew fainter as he moved away and her cries soon faded away to nothing. All Jonathan could hear now was the sound of the river, rushing toward the sea.

Wearily, he laid his cheek against Moose and tried not to cry.

Moose barked. Jonathan raised his head and looked. Moonlight glinted off the black water, making it look like liquid silver. A baby's high chair floated past, its wooden tray tilted up, as if the baby had just been lifted out. Moose barked again, wagging his tail at the high chair.

"It's okay, boy," Jonathan said. "It's only a high chair." He wondered if Moose associated the high chair with Abby. She had used one until she was almost three. Did Moose remember that?

Shore seemed farther away than it had when he floated past Beaverville. He should have left Abby then, he thought; he should have tried to swim to shore, rather than staying with her. Now they were separated anyway and the farther he was from shore, the slimmer his chance of making it.

Even if he did make it, he would not be near a town, so there weren't likely to be any people to help him. By the time the river passed Kendra, he might be even farther offshore; too far offshore to be heard, or seen.

He wondered where his parents were.

Jonathan shivered. His clothes and shoes were soaked and the cold river water continually splashed over his back as he clung to the tree trunk.

He pressed his cheek into the tree's rough bark and closed his eyes to hold back the tears. What were his chances of survival if he managed to stay on the tree and ride it all the way to the Pacific Ocean? How long could he live without food or water? The sun would burn him mercilessly all day and the freezing water would chill him at night. And what about sharks?

No one would be searching for him at sea. Rescuers would take one look at where Magpie Island used to be and assume that Jonathan and Abby had perished there.

Maybe, he thought, I should try to swim to shore now. Maybe I shouldn't wait until I pass Kendra. Once on shore, I could hike to town. Without Abby, I can walk as far as I have to.

What if I don't make it to shore?

Was it better to die trying to save himself or should he lie here hoping someone else might see or hear him?

What about Moose? Could the dog swim that far? If Jonathan tried to make it, Moose would have to try, too.

"Good dog," Jonathan said. A lump swelled his throat. "Can you make it, boy?" Jonathan whispered. "Can you swim to shore?" He reached forward and rubbed Moose's neck.

Moose turned his head and whined. Jonathan recognized the noise as Moose's hunger whine; the dog did it promptly at six every night unless Jonathan fed him before then.

I'm hungry, too, Jonathan realized. Moving slowly so as not to lose his balance, Jonathan reached over his shoulder and opened the backpack. He removed the remaining two sandwiches. He broke one in pieces and held the pieces where Moose could reach. The dog ate greedily but stayed in place.

Jonathan ate the second sandwich himself and then ate a few pieces of broken cookie. Chocolate, he knew, was not good for dogs so he didn't offer Moose any of the cookie.

When he finished eating, he looked toward shore again. It was barely visible now, even though the half moon was high in the sky. I'm drifting farther from land all the time, he thought. If I'm going to swim for shore, I must do it now.

He considered putting the leash on Moose, to be sure they stayed together, but decided against it. It wouldn't be fair, he thought, to keep the dog tied to my wrist. Moose might make it to shore, even if I don't. He buckled the leash around his own waist so he would have it later, on land.

He removed the backpack containing his mother's shoe and dropped the pack into the river. Sorry, Mom.

He inhaled deeply three times, filling his lungs with oxygen and holding it before he exhaled. His baseball coach had taught him to do that just before his turn to bat, as a way to steady his nerves.

After inhaling the fourth time, he let go of the tree and rolled sideways into the river, blowing the air out his mouth as he dropped.

As soon as his head popped up, he called, "Come, boy! Come, Moose!"

Moose was already in the water. His head and the ridge of his back were visible; his tail floated behind him as he dog-paddled beside Jonathan.

Jonathan swam toward shore, trying to establish a kicking rhythm that would keep him moving but not exhaust him. He alternated between doing the crawl, which was fastest, and the breaststroke, which was slower but allowed him to see where he was going and to see what else was floating toward him.

Moose stayed at his side, swimming as fast as Jonathan but never any faster.

Once, Jonathan changed from crawl to breaststroke just in time to see a huge tree rushing toward him. Jonathan dove under the water, coming up on the other side of the tree. Moose dove, too. After that, Jonathan stayed with the breaststroke, changing to a dog paddle when he got tired.

He looked frequently to his right, to see if anything else was floating toward him, and glanced occasionally to his left, at Moose. Two more times, he had to dive beneath the surface to avoid being hit by floating trees or parts of trees.

After ten minutes of steady swimming, a huge stump swept past him, its roots extended like outstretched hands. Jonathan grabbed one of the roots and rode along for a few seconds, resting. It occurred to him that if his strength gave out before he reached shore, he could always hang on to a different tree or another stump or something else that was floating. One way or another, he would stay alive.

Determination gave him a fresh burst of energy. He let the stump roots slip out of his grasp, and began paddling toward shore again.

His legs and arms ached. He wondered if he should have taken off his shoes before he started to swim. His feet felt like blocks of cement when he kicked. He could still get his shoes off, if he wanted to, but he would need shoes when he got to shore. He was not used to going barefoot and he would doubtless have a long hike ahead of him, once he reached land.

Land. How far had he come? When he looked, it did not seem any closer than when he first rolled off his tree. The swift current kept him going west; he could not tell if he was also moving north, toward shore.

Shoes won't do me any good if I don't make it to shore, he thought. Holding his breath, he quit kicking, reached down, and tried to untie one shoe. He sank as his cold fingers fumbled with the wet laces.

When he got the shoe untied, he swam back to the surface and dog-paddled while he used his other foot to pry the shoe off. Then he repeated his actions with the second shoe.

Each time he felt a shoe slip off his foot and sink in to the river, his heart sank, too. He knew how much he would need those shoes later, if he made it to land.

If . . .

His chest hurt from the exertion. Water splashed into his face and his father's voice echoed inside his mind: "Never drink from a river, Jonathan. Even water that looks clear and clean could be polluted." Jonathan sputtered, trying to spit it out.

He stroked toward shore.

He was tired before he started swimming. He was exhausted now. He closed his eyes and did the dead man's float, to rest. I'll float for thirty seconds, he told himself. No longer. He began to count: one, one-thousand; two, one-thousand.

Twenty seconds into his rest, something bumped his feet. Jonathan's eyes flew open as he jammed his feet down and began to tread water. A capsized tent floated past, its metal poles twisted like a pretzel. Had there been another camper on Magpie Island, after all? Jonathan wondered. Or had the tent come from the beach park in Beaverville or somewhere else?

He forced his weary body to keep swimming. Images flashed through Jonathan's mind as he swam. Bits of his past appeared in slow motion, the way television sports replays are sometimes shown. Each segment lasted less than a second, yet he clearly experienced every detail.

He saw himself as a toddler, sitting on Grandma Whitney's lap while she read him a story. He felt her warm arms around him, heard her soothing voice, and smelled a hint of talcum powder. For that brief instant, Jonathan felt secure and comforted.

Next he relived the day Abby was born and felt the excitement of going to the hospital to meet his baby sister.

He saw the tears on his mother's face and heard the fear in his father's voice two years later when they told him Abby had fallen from a slide at the playground and damaged her spinal cord. Jonathan had often thought how different his life would be if Abby's baby-sitter had not allowed her to climb alone to the top of the big slide.

The image, like the others, quickly faded and was replaced by his Little League coach, Mr. Welch. Jonathan remembered his despair after he struck out with the bases loaded. He had wanted to quit the team right then, and give up baseball forever. "Never give up, Jonathan," Mr. Welch said. "You'll have your turn to shine, as long as you keep trying. You must always keep trying." And two innings later, Jonathan smacked a triple into left field that scored the tying run.

Yes, Jonathan thought, as he pulled his arms through the water. Yes, I will keep trying.

He had heard that when people drown, they see their whole life flash before their eyes, just before they go under for the final time. Is that why he was remembering his past? Because he was almost out of strength?

He tried to kick harder but his weary legs did not respond.

Moose swam lower in the water now. His back and tail were no longer above the surface; only his head was visible. He's tired, too, Jonathan realized. He's having just as much trouble as I am.

"Good dog," he said. "Good Moose. Keep trying, boy."

The shore seemed closer. Jonathan realized the river was passing a small bay, where the land curved toward him for a time.

A shot of adrenaline burst through him, giving him new energy. He swam harder, kicking faster. If he could get out of the main current here, by the bay, he knew he would make it to shore.

He switched back to the crawl. Even though he couldn't watch for floating debris that way, it was a faster stroke. He closed his eyes, concentrating on lifting each arm over his shoulder and stroking it back as hard as he could.

He never saw the tree stump. It came toward him, spinning slightly, and hit him in the head.

Jonathan's feet quit kicking. His arms dangled limply downward. He floated briefly, face down, before he sank.

CHAPTER THIRTEEN

By the time Mr. Palmer found the high school, he was so weary that he could barely put one foot in front of the other. He stood inside the door of the gymnasium and looked quickly around.

Families sat on blankets on the floor, sipping coffee and cocoa and nibbling on doughnuts. Small children slept on cots. Beside him, a line of people snaked away from a table with a Red Cross sign hanging over it. Murmuring voices provided a steady hum in the background.

Another sign said *Emergency Medical Care.* Teams of doctors and nurses were tending various injuries.

At the far end of the gym, under one of the basketball

hoops, Mr. Palmer saw a group of people in National Guard uniforms. They, too, had a table and a line of people.

Mr. Palmer threaded his way across the gym floor. Ignoring the waiting line of people, he went directly to the National Guard table and said, "I have an emergency. Who do I need to see?"

The man at the front of the line said, "We all have emergencies tonight, Buddy. The end of the line is back there."

"I'm sorry to cut in," Mr. Palmer said, "but I need a search-and-rescue team immediately. My children were alone on Magpie Island when the earthquake hit."

The expression on the man's face changed from antagonism to concern. "Your kids were alone?" he said. "On the island?"

The National Guard officer at the table said, "The island flooded. It's gone."

"I know," Mr. Palmer said. "But Jonathan and Abby may have found a way to stay afloat. Jonathan's very resourceful. We need to send search planes, to look for them."

The officer said, "How old are they?"

"Jonathan's twelve and Abby is six," Mr. Palmer said. "She was in an accident and can't walk unassisted but Jonathan would help her. Our dog was with them, too."

A woman in the line grumbled, "He leaves a handicapped six-year-old alone and then wants special treatment to find her."

Mr. Palmer wiped the sweat from his brow. "My wife broke her ankle," he said. "She's still in our car, back by the bridge. We only left Jonathan and Abby so that I could get my wife to the hospital quickly. Please! I can explain what happened later. Right now, we need to send someone to look for my children."

"We can't send a search plane out until daylight," the officer said.

"Daylight!" Mr. Palmer cried. "That's hours from now."

"I'm sorry," the officer said and Mr. Palmer could tell by the look in the man's eyes that he was sincere. "If we knew approximately where the kids were, we'd send a search copter with a spotlight. But your kids could be anywhere between where Magpie Island was and the Pacific Ocean. That's too much territory to search in the dark."

Mr. Palmer wanted to shout, "No, it isn't!" He wanted to pound on the table and demand that every National Guard person in the state immediately set off to hunt for Jonathan and Abby.

Instead, he said, "Is there anything that can be done now?"

"If you'll step over here, Sir, we'll get all the information. We'll have a search team ready to leave at dawn."

Mr. Palmer struggled to stay calm as he answered the questions. He told how old Jonathan and Abby were, what clothes they were wearing, and gave a description of Moose.

The final question was, "How can we contact you tomorrow?"

"I'd like to go along," Mr. Palmer said, "to help look."

"I'm afraid that's against regulations."

"Then I'll be here, waiting."

There was nothing more to be done. Mr. Palmer thanked the guardsmen for their help and walked out of the gym. He would spend the night with the young man, Kenny, and his chain saw, clearing the road so he could drive his wife into town.

Abby stopped crying. Her nose was stuffed up and her head ached and she had no tears left. Periodically, she drew a long, shuddering breath. Her teeth chattered.

I want Mommy, she thought, for the hundredth time. I want to go home. I want Raggedy. I want Jonathan to come back. I want, I want, I want. . . .

But even as she yearned for help from her family, she knew they were unable to give it to her. They were not here. Not Mommy. Not Daddy. Not Jonathan.

The rough bark of the tree had rubbed her cheek raw. Abby touched her face gingerly, wondering if the wetness she felt was river water or tears or blood.

This dumb old Charlotte boat wasn't sailing forward any longer; it was only bobbing up and down.

She braced one hand on the tree and pushed her chest up. Then Abby sat up, straddling the tree. Squinting, she looked in all directions.

She was drifting in a small inlet, surrounded on three sides by land. The shore was much closer than she had expected. Even in the dark, she could clearly see trees and the outline of a cabin.

If I could swim, she thought, I could make it to shore.

But she couldn't swim. She couldn't even float.

The river splashed around her legs. Abby lay back down, clinging to the tree.

The image of the cabin stayed in her mind. She would be safe there, and dry. It would be warmer, out of the wind. Maybe there were people in the cabin, and hot cocoa to drink.

Abby began to paddle with the hand closest to shore, pushing the water, trying to propel her tree forward. She leaned over the side, plunging her arm in past the elbow to try to get as much force as possible. Her fingertips touched bottom.

Shocked, Abby leaned farther, stretching her hand downward. Yes! The water was shallow enough that her fingers grazed pebbles and sand. If I had my walker, Abby thought, I could make it to shore.

But she did not have her walker and without it, she knew she could not stay upright.

Could she crawl to shore? Maybe. But the water might be over her head if she lay on her stomach.

The only way to find out if the water was too deep was to let go of Charlotte and slip into the river. Once she got off the tree, she knew she would not be able to get back on unassisted.

She stuck her hand into the water again. This time, she did not touch bottom. The riverbed must be uneven.

Abby shivered in the dark. Jonathan had told her to stay

on Charlotte, no matter what happened. But Jonathan didn't know she was going to drift so close to shore. And anyway, Jonathan had left her behind all alone so he wasn't her boss any more.

She looked at the cabin. She tried to imagine herself in the river, crawling toward shore. If the water was too deep, she would have to hold her breath until she crawled to a shallow place.

Abby shuddered at the thought of water all around her while she crawled. But how else would she get to shore?

Land was so close.

Abby closed her eyes and scrunched up her nose, trying to decide what to do.

Abby shifted her legs off the tree on the side away from shore. Clinging to the tree trunk with both arms, she let her feet dangle downward. Her heart pounded in her chest and she held her breath as her ankles swung freely through the water. Slowly, she let her stomach slide off the tree, feeling the water creep up to her waist. The water reached her armpits before her toes touched bottom.

Abby tilted her head back and stared upward at the moon. She moved one foot forward and set it down. Then the other foot.

Pushing the tree in front of her and using it for balance, as if it were her walker, Abby walked slowly toward shore. To her surprise, her legs *did* move better underwater. Despite the cold, a warm flush of satisfaction spread through her.

She pushed the tree until the water was only waist-high.

She could see the cabin clearly now. She kept going until the river came only to her hips, and she had to bend over too far in order to hold on to the tree.

By then the remaining branches of her tree had hit bottom.

I'll have to crawl the rest of the way, Abby thought. She inched sideways until her hands were at the roots of the tree.

Good-bye, Charlotte.

She shoved the tree to her left. At the same time, she held her breath and fell face forward into the water. She bent her arms and spread her fingers so that she landed on the length of her arms from her palms to her elbows. As soon as she felt the river bottom on her arms, she straightened her elbows, pushing her head upward.

The water brushed her chin. For a moment she panicked, feeling the water surround her. I want Mommy! she thought, but she knew Mommy wasn't there. No one could save her except herself.

She tipped her head back so her face was toward the sky; her hair floated on the water. She remained motionless on her hands with her body stretched out for a long moment, slowly believing that the water was not going to hurt her.

She took a big breath and held it. Eyes closed, she bent her arms until her elbows touched bottom. As the water swirled over her head, Abby crawled forward. Right arm, left arm, right. Her legs dragged behind her across the gravelly river bottom.

She straightened her arms and put her head up for air. The water level was below her shoulders. When she bent her arms and began to crawl again, her head stayed above water.

She moved her right arm forward, and then her left. The gravel scraped her skin, but she could do it! She could crawl out of the river!

"Watch me!" she wanted to shout. "Mommy! Daddy! Look at me!" She did not shout, because there was no one to hear her, but the thrill of accomplishment propelled her forward, even without an appreciative audience.

Right arm. Left arm. Just like the Marines. Abby crawled triumphantly out of the river and lay, panting, on the shore.

She was too cold to rest. She longed to be home, wrapped in the patchwork quilt that always lay on the end of the sofa. She wanted Daddy to pick her up in his strong arms and carry her to the sofa. She wanted Mommy to tuck the quilt around her and hand her a cup of steaming cocoa. She wanted Jonathan to sit beside her and read her a story—one of her favorites like *Go, Dog, Go* or *Martha Speaks*.

Wearily, Abby forced herself back up on her forearms and dragged herself across the shore toward the dark cabin.

When she got there, she pounded on the door with her fist. There was no answer. She was not surprised, since there were no lights on inside. She really didn't care if there were people here or not. All she wanted was a warm, dry place to sleep.

She stretched her arm up, barely able to reach the doorknob. She tried to turn it.

The door was locked.

Abby huddled beside the empty cabin. "Mommy!" she yelled.

She listened, hearing the slap, slap of the river licking the shore. She did not call again.

Her stomach growled. I want toast, Abby thought, and some applesauce, and my chocolate cupcake. Jonathan promised I could have cupcakes.

She shivered again, her teeth chattering.

Maybe the cabin had a back door that was unlocked. Slowly, she crawled to the corner of the cabin, turned, and made her way along the side of the building. The ground was covered with pebbles; her arms hurt when she leaned on them and her legs, dragging behind, got more scrapes.

There was no back door.

Frustrated, exhausted, and scared, Abby curled into a tight little ball, as close to the cabin as she could get, and fell asleep.

CHAPTER

FOURTEEN

Five miles downstream from the old fishing pier, the icy water surrounded Jonathan, pushing him down as it chilled his body. Unconscious, he sank slowly.

Moose swam steadily nearby. As the water washed over the boy, the dog changed direction. Instead of continuing north, toward shore, he turned and swam east, straight against the current.

He kept his muzzle pointed up and paddled hard, forcing his head into the air. He looked toward where Jonathan had been. He saw only the river, rushing relentlessly toward him.

The dog dived under the surface. Nose down, he searched the water for his friend.

Jonathan dropped, unresisting, toward the bottom of the

river. His arms and legs hung down and his eyes were closed.

Moose saw the boy beneath him and dove deeper. He clamped his jaws on Jonathan's shoulder, sinking his teeth through Jonathan's T-shirt and into the boy's flesh, just far enough to get a good grip. Then, using every bit of strength he had, he swam upward, pulling the boy toward the surface.

Pain shot through Moose's chest as he went too long without air. He struggled on, his neck aching from the weight he dragged.

He did not make it. The boy was too heavy for the dog. Moose had to let go or be sucked under himself. He opened his mouth and released Jonathan.

The boy started to sink again.

Moose pointed his muzzle up, inhaling deeply when he burst above the surface. As soon as he had air, he dived under again. This time he swam deeper, until he was below Jonathan.

When he was completely under the boy, Moose swam upward. His head hit Jonathan's chest. Moose pushed, paddling furiously. He moved his paws as if he were climbing a ladder, and forced Jonathan's body up until Jonathan's head broke the surface. Jonathan gasped instinctively, gulping air. He choked and coughed as the oxygen rushed into his lungs, but he did not regain consciousness.

Moose swam out from under Jonathan, filling his own lungs with air.

Without the dog beneath him, holding him up, Jonathan's head splashed back into the river.

As the boy sank for the second time, Moose dove under

again. He swam beneath Jonathan, placed the top of his head on Jonathan's chest, and again pushed up. Swimming frantically, he forced the boy's head toward air.

They didn't have as far to go the second time. Jonathan surfaced before Moose was completely out of breath.

Again, the boy inhaled.

With Jonathan's face out of the water, Moose brought his own nose into the air, filling his lungs quickly. Immediately, the boy's face plunged forward into the river again.

The dog swam on, diving under every few seconds, and shoving his head against Jonathan's chest, forcing the boy's head back above water.

Each time he had his head under Jonathan, Moose faced north. As Jonathan surfaced, he was propelled forward, toward shore.

Each time Jonathan's head emerged from the river, he choked. He coughed and sputtered, swallowing large gulps of river water.

When Moose pushed him above the surface for the fifth time, Jonathan coughed again and opened his eyes. He felt something solid beneath his breastbone. Something was under him, shoving him up.

This time, Jonathan lifted his head unaided, gasping for air. His arms thrashed wildly, pushing at the river.

The pressure left Jonathan's chest and Moose's head popped above the surface a few feet from Jonathan's face. Jonathan realized Moose had been under him, pushing him out of the water.

Jonathan bent his knees and pushed, kicking his legs like

a frog. His toes tingled, as if his feet had fallen asleep from being in the same position too long. Jonathan kicked harder; the blood began to circulate again in his legs.

He raised one arm over his head and stroked toward shore. As the other arm came up, he quit frog-kicking and began to flutter his feet, settling into a steady swimmer's crawl.

Moose dog-paddled beside him, his snout pointed straight ahead, as if knowing the crisis was over for now.

Jonathan's chest hurt. River water streamed from his nose, and his head pounded with a dull aching throb. Even without touching it, he knew there was a large bump on his head. Several times he coughed hard, expelling water, but he kept swimming.

When he could breath evenly again, without coughing, Jonathan treaded water for a moment and looked toward shore. Land was still a long way off, and he was tired. Tired and cold.

I won't give up, Jonathan thought, as he began swimming again. I'll keep trying as long as there's breath in my body.

He didn't know if he would make it or not, but he did know one thing. He knew one thing for certain.

Moose had saved his life.

Abby woke crying. Her legs hurt. Her back ached. Her damp clothes clung to her shivering body, and her stomach grumbled. It took several seconds to realize where she was. When she knew, she cried harder.

Until now, the worst days of Abby's life had been her regular visits to Children's Hospital. She hated the needle they always stuck in her arm, to withdraw blood, and all the strangers in white coats moving her legs and giving her orders. Bend your knees, roll over. Do this. Do that.

But this, Abby decided, was even worse than the hospital. At the hospital, at least they fed her. Now she was so hungry she would even eat cooked carrots without gagging.

Abby rubbed the tears from her cheeks and shifted position, trying to get comfortable. She wanted to go home, and sleep in her own bed. She wished Mommy and Daddy would hurry up and come and take her home.

The horrible truth suddenly occurred to her: Mommy and Daddy can't come and get me because they don't know where I am. They think I'm in the camper and when I'm not there, they won't know where to look for me. No one knows where to look for me. Not even Jonathan.

Abby lay still, absorbing the knowledge that her whereabouts were unknown to the rest of the world.

I will have to help myself, Abby decided. But how? Without her walker, there was no hope that she could make it to a town.

Maybe she should have done what Jonathan told her to do, and stayed on her Charlotte boat. Maybe she should crawl back to the river and look for her boat and try to get back on it.

If Jonathan sent someone to help her, they would be looking for her on the tree, in the water. They wouldn't look behind this empty cabin.

The thought of going back into the cold, dark river made Abby shudder. What if she didn't make it to her boat? What if the water went over her head before she found something to hang on to?

She decided to wait until daylight. If no one had found her at the cabin by morning, she would return to the river. She would crawl into the cold, dark water and look for her Charlotte boat.

CHAPTER FIFTEEN

A National Guard helicopter rose at dawn and headed south, toward the Tuscan River. A pilot and two medics were on board.

As they neared the river, they saw total destruction below them. Great crevices had opened in the Earth's surface. Half the cars on a freight train had been knocked off the tracks and lay with their bellies in the air, like helpless turtles.

"This is a wild goose chase," the pilot said.

"We agree," one of the medics replied. "But we need to go. If we don't, one of us will have to tell Mr. Palmer that we didn't bother to look for his kids."

"You have to feel for that guy," the second medic said. "I can't imagine losing one of my kids, much less both of them at the same time. I wonder how his wife is taking it."

"There's the bridge," the pilot said. "What's left of it."

The medics looked down where Magpie Island used to be, and shook their heads. Below them, they saw only the rushing water of the Tuscan River.

"I expected the tops of trees would still stick out of the water," the pilot said.

"Maybe any trees still standing after the earthquake were washed out by the river. That water is moving."

They continued to look down. Uprooted trees, a telephone pole, and the shingled roof of a small shed floated in the water behind the downed section of the bridge, trapped against the steel girder that now angled into the river.

The Tuscan had flooded farther upstream, too, washing out several homes. A child's wooden swingset, with the slide pointing straight up, floated past the broken Magpie Island bridge.

"No kids are down there, that's for sure," the pilot said as he headed the helicopter west, following the river. "Nothing but junk in the water."

"At least we can tell Palmer we looked," one medic said. "We tried to find them."

The helicopter passed Beaverville, where a dark cloud of smoke from the previous night's fires hovered over the town.

The three men followed the shoreline, past a cove where an old fishing pier jutted into the water. Trees and other debris bobbed in the cove, away from the current. They looked down at an abandoned fishing cabin but saw no sign of life.

The helicopter noise woke Abby. She blinked, remembering where she was and why. As she realized what the noise was, excitement rushed through her. They'll help me, she thought. The helicopter will take me to Mommy and Daddy.

She looked up, toward the noise, but could not see the chopper. She was too close to the back of the cabin, and the noise came from out over the river.

If I can't see them, they can't see me, she realized. I have to crawl back to the beach. I have to get out in the open.

She rolled on to her stomach and put her arms under her shoulders, elbows bent. Her limbs were stiff from sleeping on the ground, and she could not crawl as fast as she had the night before.

The roar of the helicopter grew louder; she knew it was directly in front of the cabin.

Abby flung her arms forward, pulling herself as fast as she could. She rounded the corner of the cabin and headed toward the edge of the river.

"Here I am!" Abby screamed, but the helicopter had already flown on. She watched as it continued along the riverbank, growing smaller, until the noise died away.

Tears of frustration rolled down Abby's face and dripped onto the ground. It isn't fair! she thought. If I could run like other kids, I would have been out in the open in time. I could have run down the shore, waving my arms. They would have seen me.

Maybe it will come back, Abby thought. Maybe if she stayed out here on the shore, where she could be seen, the people in the helicopter would spot her on their way home.

It would be fun to ride in a helicopter.

She wondered if Jonathan was still on his boat. How far would he have gone by now? A long way, Abby decided. Maybe even all the way to Iowa, where Grandma Whitney lives.

Her stomach hurt. Her arms hurt. Her head hurt. *I want to go home,* Abby thought, but she blinked back her tears, knowing it did no good to cry.

I'll sing, she decided. I'll sing until the helicopter people come back and get me. She struggled to a sitting position, with her legs straight out in front of her. "You are my sunshine," she began. "My only sunshine."

The waves lapped a rhythmic accompaniment and, far in the distance, a sea gull cried.

The helicopter continued on to Kendra, where the smokestacks of a paper mill normally puffed gray clouds into the sky, twenty-four hours a day. That day, the smokestacks stood cold and empty.

"Seems funny to see the paper mill closed," the pilot said and then added, "With no electricity, the whole county is closed."

"The main road through Kendra buckled," one medic said, as he peered through his binoculars. "I see three toppled cars and a big gap down the middle of the street, like somebody opened a giant zipper."

"Wait a minute!" the other medic said. "Look down there, right on the edge of the water. Is that a person, lying on the sand?" He pointed. "See that yellow blob? Right there?"

The helicopter circled back for another look.

The second medic swung around and aimed his binoculars where the first man pointed. "It's a dog," he said. "A dead dog washed up on shore."

"It isn't dead. It moved."

"You're right. It's getting up. Wait! There's a body, too. The dog was lying on top of a person."

"A small person," the first medic said.

"I'm taking it down," the pilot said. "There's room to land between the water and the edge of the trees."

"It's a kid," the first medic said, as they descended. His voice rose. "It has to be one of those Palmer kids. The father said they had a dog with them."

The other medic continued to look through the binoculars. "The kid," he said, "isn't moving."

Jonathan lay stomach down, his cheek resting on the wet pebbles. The noise of the helicopter filled his head. Beside him, Moose barked his warning bark.

Jonathan struggled to open his eyes. He raised his head and tried to vomit, but there was nothing to come up. He lay back down with his eyes closed. His head felt as if someone had smashed him with a hammer.

The noise grew louder, a pulsing roar that surrounded Jonathan, pushing in on him from all sides. A strong wind from the chopper blades blew across him, making him shiver.

Moose's bark was frantic now.

Jonathan groaned.

He heard voices shouting.

"He moved! He's alive!"

"Hurry!"

Hands probed him gently, feeling his neck and back. They rolled him over, tilted his chin up, and swabbed out his mouth. A blanket went over his legs, bringing welcome warmth.

"Good dog," one of the voices said. "You're a fine, loyal dog."

"Look at that goose egg on his head," another voice said.

Dimly, Jonathan was aware that his blood pressure was being taken, that his arms and legs were being checked by someone obviously trained in medical procedures.

"Can you hear me?" one of the medics asked. "Are you Jonathan Palmer?"

Jonathan's eyes fluttered open. "Yes," he whispered.

"Your dad is going to be mighty glad to see you, son. And glad to see your dog, too."

"We're going to put you on a stretcher now," the other

medic said. "We'll airlift you to the hospital in Kendra. It's functioning with generators."

Jonathan licked his lips and struggled to speak. "Moose," he said.

"He's worried about the dog."

"Don't you fret about that dog, son," the first medic said. "Your dog is going for a helicopter ride, too, and after we get you to the hospital, we'll see that the dog is returned to your dad."

The voices continued, explaining to Jonathan what they were doing. "We're going to put you in the chopper now," one said.

The stretcher was lifted and Jonathan felt himself carried along the riverside. When they reached the helicopter, the stretcher was tilted at an angle as he was lifted through the opening.

Jonathan looked at the pilot.

"We never thought we'd be taking you in alive," the pilot said.

"Alive and in remarkably stable condition," a medic said. "I think the dog laid on top of him, and kept him warm."

Jonathan closed his eyes again. All he wanted to do was sleep.

Moose was boosted into the helicopter. Moose licked Jonathan's face. Jonathan smiled but did not try to wake up. He was floating in a halfway state between dreaming and being aware of where he was. He was so sleepy.

The pilot opened a bag and took out a bagel. "Here you go, dog," he said. "Have some breakfast."

Moose chomped down the bagel, wagging his tail.

The pilot said, "What happened to your sister? Do you have any idea where she is?"

Abby. Jonathan tried to concentrate but he was so tired. What had happened to Abby? She was singing, he thought. She was riding a boat and singing "Ninety-nine Raggedy Anns on the Shelf."

"Try to remember, Jonathan. Try to tell us where you last saw your sister."

But Jonathan couldn't form his thoughts into words. Without answering, he sank into a deep sleep.

The helicopter rose noisily into the sky. Instead of going back along the Tuscan, the way it had come, it continued west, toward Kendra.

CHAPTER SIXTEEN

Jonathan woke up four hours later, in a hospital bed. There was a bottle suspended over his head, and clear fluid dripped from the bottle down a tube and into his left arm.

Jonathan stared for a few moments at the bottle, and then closed his eyes, remembering.

They had kept swimming, he and Moose, until Jonathan was sure each stroke was his last.

One more, he told himself, time after time. You can't give up after Moose risked his life to save you. One more stroke. One more. One more.

Twice he did the dead man's float, to rest, and both times he had to force himself to start swimming again. One more stroke.

When he absolutely could swim no longer, he raised his head, looking for a floating tree to cling to. Instead, he saw land, only a few yards away.

One more stroke. One more.

Jonathan tried to stand, and his feet touched bottom. Exhausted, he had staggered forward and collapsed on the shore.

"Jonathan?"

Jonathan opened his eyes and turned toward the voice. A woman in a white uniform approached his bed. She stuck a thermometer in his mouth, and picked up his right wrist and took his pulse.

When she removed the thermometer, she said, "How are you feeling?"

"Tired. My head hurts."

"I should think so. There's a bump the size of a baseball where something hit you. You're lucky the human body is prepared for emergencies. Have you ever heard of the diving reflex?"

Jonathan shook his head.

"The body's diving reflex allows us to survive in cold water even when we're submerged for long periods of time. The heartbeat slows and the arteries nearest the skin get smaller so that the blood carries oxygen away from your arms and legs and toward your heart and brain. In cold water, the oxygen needs of the tissues are reduced, which extends the possible time of survival. It's really quite remarkable, and the diving reflex is more active in children than in adults."

"My dog saved me," Jonathan said.

She smiled at him. "I'd better let your parents know you're awake. They're terribly worried about you."

"Where are they?"

"Your father is in Beaverville. Search parties are looking for your sister and others; he's at the search headquarters. Your mother's downstairs, in the recovery room. A young man with a four-wheel-drive vehicle brought her in, and she had surgery on her ankle this morning."

What a family, Jonathan thought.

"Rest while I call the National Guard emergency line and leave a message for your father. I'll tell the doctor you're awake, too. He'll want to check you again. And I'll send word down to your mother, though I don't imagine she's slept off the anesthetic yet."

Jonathan lay still, remembering everything that had happened. He remembered the earthquake, the river flooding, the trees that he and Abby clung to as they floated toward the ocean, singing.

Suddenly, his eyes flew open. He fumbled for the call button that hung on the headboard and pushed it. The nurse hurried back into the room.

"I remember what happened to Abby," he said. "I have to tell someone where to look for her."

Minutes later, Jonathan was connected by phone to the National Guard station in the Beaverville High School gym. His father was on the other end of the line.

"We were each riding on a tree," Jonathan said. "I know we passed Beaverville, because I saw the outline of some buildings and what looked like fires. Not too long after that, Abby's tree seemed to quit moving. It was as if she got stuck somehow or floated out of the main current. I kept going, but she didn't."

As Jonathan talked, Mr. Palmer looked at a large topographical map of the area. "Hold on a minute," he said, and turned to repeat Jonathan's words to the National Guardsman who headed the search for Abby. He pointed to a cove on the map. "Right about here," he said.

"Fish Head Bay," the guardsman said. "There's an old pier that sticks out into the river at that point. If Abby floated into the bay, she would be out of the current and would not go any farther downstream." He turned away from the map and began barking orders into a two-way radio, directing a search party to head immediately for Fish Head Bay.

"Where's Moose?" Jonathan asked, when his father returned to the telephone.

"He's here with me, getting spoiled rotten. The men who found you told everyone how Moose laid on top of you and kept you warm. Your dog's a hero; everyone's feeding him pieces of doughnut."

Jonathan smiled.

"I'll be there as soon as I can," Mr. Palmer said. "Pray for your sister."

Jonathan drifted in and out of sleep. Once, in his dreams, he relived the earthquake and woke up trembling, his hospital gown drenched with sweat.

He had no idea how much time had passed. The doctor

checked him twice. "You have a concussion," the doctor said, "and hypothermia, but you'll heal. You'll be fine in a few weeks."

A nurse came in periodically to get his vital signs.

Jonathan slept again.

"Room service," a voice beside him said.

Jonathan opened his eyes. A nurse stood beside him, holding a tray containing a cup of clear broth, a bowl of red Jell-O, and some vanilla yogurt. "Just like a fancy hotel," she said, "except you don't have to tip me."

She pushed a button and the head end of his bed went up. Although he had no appetite, he ate most of what she brought, knowing he needed nourishment to keep his strength up.

He thought about Abby, guiltily remembering all the times he had resented having to wait for her. What if Abby was never found? What if she was dead?

Jonathan could not imagine life without her.

I did the best I could, Jonathan told himself. *I kept her from being too scared; I tried to save her. I did the best I could for Abby.* But he didn't know if his best was good enough.

The needle was removed from his arm, and the bottle taken away.

Jonathan fell asleep, still sitting up. In his dreams, he heard Abby's small voice singing, "Itsy-bitsy spider."

The telephone on the bedside table rang. Jonathan jerked awake and grabbed the receiver.

"Hello?"

"They found her!" Mr. Palmer's voice boomed into Jonathan's ear. "She seems to be all right! She's being airlifted to the same hospital you're in, and I've requested that you be put in a double room together. I'll get there as soon as I can."

Two hours later, men in white uniforms rolled a gurney into Jonathan's room. The small body under the blanket lay perfectly still. The attendants unbuckled the straps that held the patient in place, and lifted her into the hospital bed.

Abby's dark hair rested on the white pillowcase. Her eyes were closed.

"Abby?" Jonathan said. "Can you hear me?"

Her eyes opened. She turned her head and stared at Jonathan.

"Hi, Abby," he said. His arms tingled with excitement. She was alive. She was awake.

"We're in the hospital," Jonathan said.

"I know. The doctor told me. Where's Mommy?"

A voice from the doorway said, "I'm right here." Mrs. Palmer entered the room in a wheelchair, her right foot and lower leg in a cast. She wheeled between the two beds, stood shakily, and leaned forward to kiss Abby. She turned and kissed Jonathan, too, before she sank back into the wheelchair. "I was so worried about you," she said, as she wiped tears of joy from her cheeks.

"We were plenty worried, too," Jonathan said.

The doctor who had examined Abby in the emergency

room arrived. "It's amazing," he said. "She has some cuts and bruises, and slight hypothermia, but that's it. We'll keep her for a day or two for observation but I anticipate no serious problems. You kids were lucky. Both of you."

A short time later, Mr. Palmer rushed into the room.

"You look as if you should be hospitalized, too," Mrs. Palmer said, after everyone had briefly explained what happened.

"All I need is a hot shower and a good night's sleep," Mr. Palmer replied.

"And some clean clothes," Jonathan said.

"How did you get here so fast?" Mrs. Palmer asked. "I heard many of the roads are still closed."

"Some are, but not all. Someone from The Red Cross drove me."

"What about Moose?" Jonathan asked.

"He's still at the emergency headquarters in the Beaverton High School. Don't worry about Moose. Half a dozen people offered to take care of him until we can get back for him. He's getting so much attention, he probably won't want to go home with us."

"I'm hungry," Abby said.

"The nurse will bring you some hot soup soon," Mrs. Palmer said. "I heard her order it."

"I don't want soup," Abby said. "Jonathan promised I could have a chocolate cupcake, and three pineapple milk shakes."

"Oh?" Mrs. Palmer raised her eyebrows.

"Soup first," Mr. Palmer said firmly.

"And then cupcakes," Abby said. "Jonathan said I can lick the wrapper."

Jonathan grinned. He was actually looking forward to those six games of *Go, Fish*.